POWELL'S #3 MISCELLANEOUS THOUGHTS AND STORIES 2020

#1 Powell's Heart In Right Place—Brain Asleep   Jan 2020

#2 Surprises in Heaven?   (My thoughts) Dec 2019

#3. Auction Medal   (Fiction) Jan 2020

#4. MRS. (DELORES) JONAH.   (Fiction)

#5. AMAZON SHIRT   (True)

#5-A   PET ROCKS FOR PRESIDENT.   (My comment) Sep 2020.

#6. HELP ME FIND SOMEONE TO HELP TODAY. (True)

7. FORGOTTEN FITBIT—LED TO HELPING LADY (True)

#8. O-MA—ONE YEAR AFTER HER DEATH

9. POWELL-AUTOBIOGRAPHY—1962   (True)

#10. CORONA VIRUS 2020

#11. SAVORING   Feb 2020   (True)

#12. CARTOON-TOY MEMORIES BY RICHARD, SHARON, BEN June 2020

#13. SINGING AND DANCING IN THE SUNSHINE (fiction) Mar 2020

#14. WAS AARON OLDER THAN MOSES?   APR 2020 (True)

#15. ROCKING HORSE WITH RUNNING BOARD (True) Apr 2020

#16. FROM WHENCE COMES THE SOUL—AND WHEN? ++ And Other ++April 2020

#17. A MILL JOB—DESPERATION TO ELATION -- May 2020   (fiction)

#18. YAHWEY'S SONG BIRD   May 2020 (fiction)

#19. POND BANK   May 2020 (true)

#20. MANKIND'S PHOENIX   May 2020 (fiction)

#21. KALAHARI Jan 2018   (fiction my rewrite)

#22. JACOB'S AND JESUS' GARDEN.   June 2020--- (Fiction)

#23. JESUS' SISTER SPEAKS (fiction) July 2020

#27. JESUS SAID, "YES, IT IS YOU" Mar 2020 (Fiction)

#28. JESUS TALKS TO JUDAS   (Fiction) June 2020

#29. YOUNG JESUS WASHES FEET (Fiction) June 2020

#30. YOUNG JESUS VISITS DEAD POND.   (Fiction) July 2020

#31. YOUNG JESUS HEALS INJURED PUPPY (Fiction) July 2020

#32. YOUNG JESUS AND JOHN GO TO GALILEE (fiction) July 2020

#33. YOUNG JESUS AND JOHN--DESERT RESCUE (fiction) July 2020

#34. YOUNG JESUS AND JOHN MEET TWO BLIND MEN (fiction) July 2020

#35. YOUNG JESUS AND JOHN DIG A WELL (Fiction) July 2020

#36 YOUNG JESUS AND JOHN—BOAT RESUCE (Fiction) July 2020

#37. YOUNG JESUS AND JOHN---LOST BOYS (Fiction) July 2020

#38. YOUNG JESUS AND JOHN—MIDWIFE (FICTION) July 2020

#39. YOUNG JESUS AND JOHN—FIREFIGHTERS (Fiction) July 2020

#40. YOUNG JESUS AND JOHN—DRIVE A CHARIOT (Fiction) July 2020

#41. YOUNG JESUS AND JOHN—OLD SHEPHERD (Fiction) August 2020

#42. YOUNG JESUS AND JOHN—WORK IN A VINEYARD (Fiction) August 2020

#43. YOUNG JESUS AND JOHN—VISIT A PRISON (Fiction) August 2020

#44. YOUNG JESUS MAKES SHOES FOR JOHN (Fiction) Aug 2020

#45. YOUNG JESUS AND JOHN— A DYING MAN (Fiction) Aug 2020

#46. YOUNG JESUS AND JOHN—BEES AND A DRUNK (Fiction) Aug 2020

#47. MARY ENCOUNTERS UNMARRIED EXPECTING GIRL (Fiction) Aug 2020

#48. YOUNG JESUS AND JOHN—WIDOW IN COURT—STONES   (Fiction) Aug 2020

#49. YOUNG JESUS AND JOHN FIND A BABY (Fiction) Aug 2020

#50. YOUNG JESUS AND JOHN—AN OLD MAN (Fiction) Aug 2020

#51. YOUNG JESUS AND JOHN—PUPPIES   (Fiction) Aug 2020

#52. YOUNG JESUS AND JOHN—LATE TO THE HARVEST (Fiction)   Sep 2020

#53. YOUNG JESUS AND JOHN AT A WEDDING (Fiction) Sep 2020

#54. YOUNG JESUS AND JOHN—JAMES JOINS THEM IN THE WILDERNESS (Fiction) Sep 2020

#55. YOUNG JESUS AND JOHN—TWO ORPHANS-- PIGGYBACK. (Fiction) Sep 2020

#56. YOUNG JESUS AND JOHN—A PATCH OF FLOWERS AND A PINNACLE (Fiction) Sep 2020

#57. YOUNG JESUS SAVES A BOY'S PET SHEEP (Fiction) Sep 2020

#58.

#67. YOUNG JESUS AND JOHN VISIT ONE OF THE WISE MAN (Fiction) August 2020.

#68. YOUNG JESUS AND JOHN—LAST TRIP TOGETHER TO DESERT (Fiction) Aug 2020

#69. JESUS AT HIS 30TH BIRTHDAY. (Fiction) August 2020

#70.   JESUS IN MY DREAM (TRUE) July 2020

#71. CORN STORAGE IN-GROUND—OLD MEMORY (True) July 2020

#72. JOE LIGHTSEY—VIETNAM VET AND QUIET HERO (True) Aug 2020

#73. MY BAPTISM (True) Aug 2020

#74. ALWAYS ASK THE QUESTION. June 2020 (True) (PPP Stopper list exception)

#75. JOB HOPPER June 2020 (True)

#76. I NEED MY EDUCATION.   (True) June 2020

#77.   MEMORIES BY RYLEE FOR O+PA JUNE 2020 (True)

#78. Our little POPPY GIRL   Sept 10, 2020

#79 A daily prayer: OH LORD: HELP ME TO LOVE YOU MORE. Etc. Sep 2020

#80. MOVING A METAL CARPORT (True) Sep 2020

#81. RAISING A SMALL METAL SHED (True) Oct 2020

#82. PUSHING BATTERY-POWERED WHEELCHAIR—GOD'S TIMING (True) 2 Oct 2020

#83. MY HAIR IS LONGER THAN YOURS! YAAAH! PRAISE THE LORD!   (True) Sep 2020

#84. MISS VERNA ALLISON - My favorite teacher By Jack Christopher (True) Oct 2020

#85.

+++

#1. POWELL'S HEART IN RIGHT PLACE—BRAIN ASLEEP   Jan 2020 (True)

Background: Most weekdays I go to the Houston Health Pavilion to walk and usually enter through the same door— East #1, but have never paid attention to the door's number. One day as I neared some double doors to the main walking area, I saw a limping lady with a cane and purse so I sped up to hold the door for her. I thought she had entered through the South #1 door. We chatted a bit. She was going to a thyroid doctor so I suggested she see the information volunteer at the desk. Later I asked if he helped and she said no as she went west and later I saw her lean on the wall to rest and ask someone else for information and she headed toward a doctor's office on the East 3 hall. Trying to attain 10,000 steps each day takes about an hour and a half or more so I was still there when I saw her outside East 3 parking lot looking for her car or ride. Later she was seated at East 3 waiting so we chatted and I told her this was not the door she came in and she said "It's not?" Told her to wait till I could get a wheel chair for her, which I did and pushed her to South #1. She did not have her cell but knew her brother's number which we called on mine, he was at East #1 waiting for her. ((Comment: They were at different doors waiting for each other. Guess it was good that God had me notice—though as you will see, I didn't handle it very efficiently. Thank you Lord for letting me help someone.))

Here's where my brain was asleep. Somehow I thought East #1 must be at the far end of the Pavilion (still haven't figured that one out). So pushed her all the way down to the far end only to discover that was East #5. Went through that door, outside, headed back by East 4, 3, and finally East # 1, my daily door. Finally my brain woke up. We called her brother again and he stepped outside and they were reunited.

I am still laughing at myself. I hope Jesus is too and maybe He is thinking—his heart is in the right place but his brain was asleep. I ended yesterday laughing and started today laughing, so my sleep brain served a good purpose.   Hope I can help someone every day.

+++

#2. SURPRISES IN HEAVEN?   Dec 2019   (My thoughts)

Maybe some of the surprises in heaven will be that we will get to look back at our entire life and see the unbelievable number of times and events where God was there looking after us and guiding us and directing other events and people to be in just the right place at just the right time (perhaps even delayed) for our benefit. I can imagine us saying Oh I didn't know You did that for me--I thought it just happened or I just thought I'd always been lucky.

If I'd gotten what I wanted that's what would have happened? Thank You God.

Oh, You were there in the dark times too--I thought I was so alone--I could barely keep going--but I see now You were the One that kept picking up my feet and kept pushing me until I was out of the dark valley.   Sort of like "Footprints in the Sand", You carried me many times.

And You arranged for me to meet her--and You made sure she saw me instead of that other guy --he was taller and better looking, glad he somehow went the other way oh-- You again.

You were there with our children--wow--every time--each and every day and night--Thank You. And the Grands too.

I should have known--You were always there--always. Thank You, Thank You, Thank You….

++++++++++++++++++++++++++

3. __AUCTION MEDALS__ Jan 2020 (fiction)

As they stopped for gas at the remote general store, they read the note advertising an auction at the end of Lincoln Line—everything must go. She asked to go but he said they'd taken the back roads and he'd wasted enough time but she asked again and he gave in—grumpily. She smiled and said remember your uncle says, "delays often lead to blessings."

They went in different directions at the farm auction. He wandered up to the porch where the old man sat rocking. He said 30 years of farming, 30 years of heart ache, 30 years of day to day and hard work. I'm even selling these Army medals.

When he saw the Medals he did a double take—there were purple hearts, a silver star and a Congressional Medal of Honor. He asked if he could read the citation for the Congressional Medal of Honor—as he read it his heart quickened. Then he shook the farmer's hand, gave him a salute and told him he had saved his dad's life—he wouldn't be alive except for his heroic deeds that day. Then he dashed off to find his wife and tell her. But in mid-stride he heard the auctioneer and rushed up to him saying the auction is over, I just bought everything.

Epilogue: In the days that followed he made arrangements for the Hero to keep the farm and even got Veteran's benefits started for him. He arranged for a reunion of all the men he had saved and their families so the Hero would know what an impact he had had on so many people.

Note: This story came after hearing Tommy New sing a song at Powersville Opry, Georgia, about an Auction . 1/2020

+++++++++++++++

++++++++++++++++++++++++++++++++

#4. MRS. (DELORES) JONAH.   Jan 2020 (fiction)

((I am a big fan of Gary Larson. I hope he doesn't mind my little silly story so much. I tried to picture my deceased wife of 52 years as Mrs. Jonah and myself as Jonah. My wife's name was Delores and she would tolerate just about anything—including me—except me drinking and seeing another woman. Here's how I thought she might react. Again, thank you Mr. Larson for all your cartoons—my mind is a little off center sometimes, so I think we would have been good friends growing up.))

Mrs. Jonah/Delores: Do you expect me to believe that story?

Jonah. Well that's what happened.

Delores: Were you drinking?

Jonah: No!

Delores: Were you with another woman?

Jonah: Smelling like this? No, never.

Delores: (Mumbling) Other than me, that's the only kind of woman that would put up with you.

Delores: Ok I believe you. Get cleaned up for supper.

Jonah: Good. After three days, I'm really hungry. What are we having?

Delores: Hush puppies and …………

Jonah: Noooooooo…………

#5. <u>**AMAZON SHIRT**</u>   Jan 2020 (True)

At WalMart, a young lady was wearing a shirt with Amazon logo. I asked if I could make a bad joke. She said go ahead. I said, I know you can order just about anything on line. Looks like your parents ordered you from Amazon. She and cashier laughed and she said that's pretty good.

((Idea: Maybe Amazon could become an adoption agency…………… Maybe I've been reading too many Far Side cartoons.)

+++++++++++++++++++++++++++++++

#5-A   <u>**PET ROCKS FOR PRESIDENT.   (My comment) Sep 2020.**</u>

For President, each party could run a pet rock and each would get 50+ million votes.

(Is that pessimism or the sad truth?   Statement would probably prompt some comments.)

+++

#6. <u>**HELP ME FIND SOMEONE TO HELP TODAY**</u>. Jan 2020 (True)

Most mornings after my devotional, my prayer includes these thoughts "help me find someone to help today." On Tuesday and Thursday's I take my friend who cannot drive to his exercise class—what a blessing of getting to know him. Weekdays I try to walk 10,000 steps at the Pavilion where I've met new walking friends (See #1 above). I often see an opportunity to hold a door for someone or maybe even help direct them to the correct doctor's office, etc. One day as I neared the exit, a man commented on my hat which is covered with pictures of my grand-darlings and my whole family. Then he explained that his apartment had burned a few days ago, he and his wife had stayed in a Budget Inn, they were out of money with nowhere to stay tonight, Budget Inn was holding their bags. He was there for a doctor's appointment. Churches and friends had helped and an uncle from Texas was coming in two days but they needed help. The room was in his wife's name. Got her name and phone number and said let me see what I can do—while they waited for appointment. I got gift card at Huddle House across street from Budget Inn and paid for 3 nights at Budget Inn, who confirmed that their bags were there. Drove back to Pavilion and they were walking toward Budget Inn, picked them up (I have a hard rule against hitchhikers—what if he had pulled a gun.) and drove them to Budget Inn. So they had a room and food till hopefully his uncle arrived. ((He said he was 55 and she had applied for SSI. I should have asked how they afforded the apartment. Apparently no income.))

So, thank you God for answering my prayer—I hope I did the right thing.

++++++++++++++++++

7. FORGOTTEN FITBIT—LED TO HELPING LADY Jan 2020 (True)

Same week, my friend forgot her fitbit when she walked at the Pavilion so did not get credit for those steps. I walked with her that afternoon so she could get fitbit credit in the amount she needed. As we walked, we noticed a limping lady who looked confused so we asked if we could help. She was in the wrong section. My friend, sweet person that she is, said drive your car to the other door and I'll be there and direct you to the right place. She went out of her way to help the lady and walked with her inside to the desk and asked if the lady was in the right place and did not leave until the lady at the desk said yes. The confused lady would have driven back to Macon and not gotten the necessary labs done. After that, as we talked,--the pieces fell into place. We realized, had my friend worn her fitbit that morning we would not have come back to the Pavilion that afternoon. We would have missed the blessing of helping that lady and she would have driven back to Macon without the lab work. So, thank you Lord for helping us help others and helping us see that our mistakes can sometimes lead to helping others.

++++++++++++++++++

#8. O-MA—ONE YEAR AFTER HER DEATH   By granddaughter Rylee Hancock Jan 27, 2020

it's been one year.

one year since you left this earth.

i never thought i'd be ok today.

this time last year my world had shattered. yes we all knew your time was coming, but when reality slaps you in the face and you realize you're loved one is gone and they're not coming back, your world literally changes.

when i learned that you left to be with Jesus, my heart stopped.

i tried to cry, but only managed a few tears. time just froze.

i thought, "In one day, how am I going to be any better? How am I going to continue on this journey of life without Oma?"

then that one day turned into one week, and I was thinking the same thing; "How will I be any better in 6 months?"

then 6 months cane and I was thinking the same thing. I had blinked and time did it's thing and I was somehow healing. I still didn't know how I could go another 6 months and be fine.

well it's been another 6 months, a total of one year without my Oma.

to tell the truth, I'm not fine. I will never be fine again. But that's okay. It's okay to not be okay. Yes I've healed but nothing will patch the hole in my heart that belonged to my dear Oma.

I miss her terribly every day. There are things I wish I could have told her, things I wish we could have done. I know she's still with me. She's with Jesus, too.

i've incorporated this into my daily prayer; "Tell Oma hello, and that I love her so much. Give her a hug for me and a kiss, and tell her I can't wait to see her again."

i miss you. we all do.

i love you, oma. 🖤

image may contain: 1 person, sitting, cat and eyeglasses

+++++++++++++++++++

#9.   POWELL—AUTOBIOGRAPHY—1962   By Donnie Powell

Autobiography my Senior Year. English 12 Mrs. Pearl S. Garrett May 16, 1962

(Note: Mrs. Garrett had us write our autography in the 11th grade and then update it in the 12th grade. So glad she required this—brought back many memories and things I had forgotten. Hope you enjoy.)

The Junior-Senior Prom Dance highlighted a wonderful Junior year for me. I escorted Joyce McCorkle to the Prom and had a wonderful time. On the way home, the police stopped us and I asked if I was going too slow.

Commencement exercises were the last of May, and since my sister Brenda Jane, was graduating, I attended all the services. The day after graduating, I received my report card, thus ending my Junior Year.

June 1961 flew rapidly past, again I spent my free time doing nothing. I even failed to read any books. I was first introduced to the great sport of tennis in June. I shortly afterward bought a tennis racket and spent many an hour of my vacation at the tennis court.

July, 1961 went much like June, with one main exception I had been awarded a week's vacation for my family and myself at Ida Cason's Callaway Gardens. We enjoyed the wonderful recreational facilities of the Gardens, mainly swimming, boat riding, and the Florida State University circus whose summer headquarters were there. I even tried skiing for the first time, I was a big splash. The week's vacation ended with a dance on Saturday night. We had round and square dancing, and I just had a ball. (Note:

Met many other students from other schools and I learned how to juggle three balls. While there, Roger Maris hit four of his 61 home runs during one double header—just happened to remember that.)

Back home, I got into the old grind of doing nothing, except taking care of Ricky, because both my parents worked.

June French, Co-Ed-Y vice president and I as Chaplain attended the YMCA leadership conference at the 4-H Center at Rock Eagle in August. I went prepared to study and learn my duties as Chaplain, but I also went to enjoy the fellowship of others my age. We had some wonderful socials, speeches, and games; and a spiritual experience which I shall never forget. June's parents were considerate and provide return transportation for us. I enjoyed the trip home even though I was slightly ill and very sleepy. (Note: One night at Rock Eagle, I was sick and took my asthma medication on an empty stomach which mace me very sick. Next morning in line for breakfast, two nice guys let me go in front of them. Later as students at Southwestern they remembered me as the "green" guy at 4-H camp.)

My senior year began on September 1, 1961. The senior sponsors were Mrs. Pearl S. Garret and Mr. Gary Simpson, the two best sponsors in school. The seniors bestowed the honor of President of the senior class upon me. It was the greatest honor I had received from my fellow students.

Besides being president of the senior class, I was Chaplain of the Co-ed-Y Club, District president of the Library Club, a member of the Future Teachers Association, and a member of the Beta Club. My subjects were as follows: first period—Typing II, Second period—English 12; third period—advanced math; fourth period—Physics; fifth period—American government; and sixth period—study hall, in which I served as a library assistant.

In October, 1961 the seniors and juniors were permitted to take the preliminary scholastic aptitude test. I took it mainly because it helps to prepare a student for the Scholastic Aptitude Tests.

October 18, 1961 was college day at Americus, which was attended by a group of seniors and juniors, myself included.

The Senior English Class of which I am a member, gave a play entitled "Punktown Court" on October 27, 1961. The play was a big success mainly because of the determination of the Seniors and because of the encouragement and guidance of Mrs. Garrett.

Senior rings arrived on October 30, 1961, making me feel that I was officially a senior.

Co-ed-Y members and officers were installed at the Baptist church on November 9.

The big day arrived. The third district west Library organization held its annual meeting in the auditorium of Marion County High and as president, I presided. I was scared but knew all the other officers were pulling for me and somehow I made it through the meeting.

Thanksgiving holidays were November 23 and 24. I enjoyed the days by quail hunting mostly.

On December 2, 1961, I was one of a number of Seniors who took the Scholastic Aptitude Test in Americus. When the scores returned, I was delightfully surprised to find that

I had a score of 590 in the math, the highest from our school, and on the verbal I received 428, about average.

December 14 saw me taking the Department of Labor Tests, which were given to Seniors to help determine their future careers.

The much awaited day of December arrived to my keen joy. The Christmas holidays began, giving me a few days rest from the burden of homework.

On January 6, Mrs. McGlaun, Librarian, and George Grier, local Library Club President, and I attended the state Library Club executive board meeting at Camp Jackson, at which meeting, plans were made for the annual state convention. I was appointed to the Careers Committee of the state educational department.

Co-ed-Y club officers were guests of the Lions club at the January 16 meeting, and everyone enjoyed a delicious meal, but afterward the officers gave a short talk on the different phases of the Y Club.

February 9 was the end of basketball season with the girls having a record of 19-4 and the boyw 21-2. I had enjoyed most of the games and also enjoyed working in the concession stand at some of the home ball games.

Admiring dancing the way I do, I naturally went to nearly every social that I could. At the FHA Valentine Social, I became a "Twist" convert and twisted at every social that I could for the rest of the year.

Beta Convention was March 9-11 in Atlanta, and along with about ten other Betas from our school, I attended. Since I was involved complications naturally resulted and things worked out so that Billy Moore and I got to see the

Marion County Red Foxes win the State Class C championship by defeating at the state tournaments, respectively: Laurens, Western, Coosa, and Jackson. The Mighty Red", had previously won the sub-region, regional and many games during the season, all with only two defeats. The Marion County Red Vixens—rather Foxetts— did their best (but the fans didn't do their best because very little support was given the girls) and got second place in the sub-regional tournaments, and third in the regional tournaments.

Allergy tests were scheduled for me starting March 26 in Atlanta. The tests took only about four hours Monday and an hour each Tuesday and Wednesday. To my keenest delight the tests were completed on Wednesday and I happily arrived homed Wednesday afternoon. (Note: My Dad arranged a ride there and back with Mr. Sonny Duncan and I appreciate his giving me a ride. He asked me what I thought about some schools closing due to integration and I'm not big and strong, so I need my education. I do not want our schools closed. He said if I needed help (financially) with schooling, to come see him (the banker). During the pollens part of the allergy tests, the nurse said my back "lit up".)

Why was I happy because a trip had ended? Was I slipping? No! For on the following day, Thursday, March 29, Mr. Charles Burger, June French, Annelle Powell, Vicki Pope and I left for the convention of the Future Teachers Association at Jekyll Island. We had interesting meetings, talks, and experiences, which were highlighted by a banquet and dance Friday night. Again, I twisted and also danced and as usual regretted the time when the last dance was over.

April seemed to stimulate the teachers for they really piled the homework upon us. Perhaps they knew that we could stand anything now that the diploma were almost within reach and getting nearer.

April 27, 28, and 29 were the dates for the annual GALA convention, which this year for the first time was held at Camp Jackson. Third District West, the one in which we are in, was in charge of souvenirs and Mrs. McGlaun and the rest really did a lot of work and a good job.

At the Ga Association of Library Assistants (GALA) convention in 1961, I had met Annette Bell and she was at the 1962 convention, so we renewed our friendship and I really had a ball. There was a dance Friday night, a banquet, and a dance Saturday night and we seldom sat a dance out. But all good things must come to an end, and I left Camp Jackson realizing that I would porbably never see the camp or Annette again.

The Senior play is one of the big events of the Senior year. I was chosen to be the cruel murderer of the play. (Quite fitting wasn't it?) Many practices and much determination, plus the encouragement and guidance of Mrs. Garrett were needed to overcome the speeches, difficulties and accidents which pertained to the play. But on May 4, the Seniors turn in an excellent performance, in my opinion, the best in the history of senior plays of our school. (Note: Doug Jones broke his ankle as he burst through a stage door and had to be replaced by Barney Miller with only a few days of practice left. Barney worked hard and did a good job. After the play, Doug told Barney, "you did a better job than I would have done"—way to go Doug.)

The Senior year's big social event, the Junior-Senior Prom Dance was help May 11. I was at first unable to get a date and had determined to go "stag" But I was lucky and had the honor of escorting classmate Diana Brannon to the Prom. The decorations were superbly beautiful (in the old gym) and the band was very good—the theme was a "Roman Holiday"—so how could anyone keep from having a good time?

The biggest event of the Senior year is of course graduation, and with graduation, Class Night which will be May 25, and the Baccalaureate sermon which will be May 27.

Each previous graduating class had had four honor graduates and the fifth highest as alternate. But since I was involved, naturally things had to be complicated. (It seems I'm always messing things up.) Shep Pryor and I were tied for fourth, so on Graduation Night, May 31, there will be five speeches. The valedictory given by Fran Brooks, the salutation given by Annelle Powell, Brenda Henson third, and Shep and I fourth. We were thrilled with the honor, but realize that with all honors come responsibilities. We are working on our speeches and will present them on graduation night, May 31, 1962.

The End (Or The Commencement)

PS—The gym, classrooms, and auditorium were NOT air conditioned.

+++++++++++++++++++++++

10. CORONA VIRUS COVID-19   2020   (True)

March 20—Day 2 of my self quarantine. New York and California just put state wide total lock down. Big 3 auto makers have shut down and many other businesses have shut down. Uncharted waters. Schools shut down. Trinity closed. Being told to social distance at least 6 feet from everyone. No hand shake or hugs. Think it will take months or longer. Some medicines promising. Scary. Had to tell my grand-darlings not to overnight on Fridays for at least 2-3 weeks—now I'm thinking it will be until they self quarantine and I mean see no body else—I'm over 60 (I'm 75) so I'm in the danger age.

March 23—Day # 5—Walked around Walkers Pond but stayed at least 6 feet away from everyone. Warner Robins and now Georgia declaring national emergencies. Ben and, I think Tommy, signing up for 60 days Admin leave—Robins may also close for some time. Stock market at 18591 (was near 30,000 a couple months ago). May be heading for Depression. Many people out of work. Italy hard hit. World wide, total cases 332, 930 and total deaths 14,509.

I've been praying "Peace. Be Still." That's what Jesus said to the storm and this Corona is a storm. I've also been praying, "I'm Yours Oh Lord. We are Yours oh Lord. Thank You for the incomprehensible privilege of being Yours. Amen.

Mar 24—Things getting worse world wide and in the US. Many businesses shut down. I walked with Kathy at Walkers. Thought about going to doctor but changed my mind. Trump/Pence doing great job. Dems in congress holding up stimulus by adding on things unrelated to helping citizens and businesses affected by virus. You'd think they could work for good of citizens.   Total cases World wide 372,757, with 16,231 deaths.

Mar 28--- In US 2000+ deaths.

April 2---US Cases   241,158—Deaths   5,827------ Recovered 10,400 (GA 5348 cases w/163 deaths)

 Apr 2---Worldwide   1.013,157—Deaths   52,983— Recovered 210,263

 Inconvenience better than Illness. Kathy and I self isolating so far #15 days (only 14 required) but we are going for 21 to be safe.   Georgia schools out for the rest of the school year. 5 cases on Robins AFB.

April 6—Until now US discouraged wearing masks. Now encouraging wearing cloth masks. Ben has 100.8 fever. Scary. Walked at Pond. #19.

Apr 7—Ben's below 98 with sore throat PTL.

+++++++++++++++++

MY THOUGHTS---Corona—Self Quarantine   24 Mar 2020

Here is what Self-quarantine means to me due to the Corona virus. By Donnie Powell 3/24/2020

I am taking these Sheltering in Place, Self Isolating, or Quarantined stringent measures to protect myself (age 75), others and especially my loved ones from getting the

Covid-19 virus from me. I consider myself potentially "contaminated" until I complete Sheltering in Place.

1. I must stay away from EVERYONE for at least 14 days and perhaps INDEFINITELY. Maybe I should have a sign "IF I TOUCH YOU, YOU MAY DIE. IF YOU TOUCH ME, I MAY DIE."

2. NOTE: I can only physically meet with someone who has been truly Self Isolated at least 14 days. If you have not truly Self Isolated, you may be taking my life in your hands, and the lives of all those you and I meet.

3. That means not within 6 feet of a doctor, friend, sales person at grocery, drug store, food pick up, etc., or any one. It is ok to walk outside but staying 6 feet away from everyone.

4. Anyone we come in contact with could be carrying the Corona virus--we must consider everyone "contaminated or unclean" (Sorry to use these words but maybe they will help drive home the seriousness of the situation. I am unclean until I self-quarantine for 14 days.)

5. If I pick up food/medicine/etc., I'll pay by credit card (prefer in advance) and pick up with gloves on and at a distance of at least 6 feet. (Hope I can work that out.)

6. If I come within 6 feet of anyone--and I mean anyone--I MUST start the 14 day Self Isolation again.

7. If I am dating, we each self-isolation separately. After 14 days we can see each other but only if we do not come within 6 feet of anyone else. If we do, we must start the 14 day self-isolation again.

8. I want to hug my daughter and her family including my two grand-darlings. But I cannot until my 14 days is over-- AND until they EACH have been sheltered in place for 14 days. If even one comes within 6 feet of someone else (becomes contaminated) they all (everyone in the house) must re-start their 14 days again.

9. We can only physically meet with someone who has been truly self isolated at least 14 days.

10. IMPORTANT: After the first 14 day true self isolation, we may need to continue sheltering in place INDEFINITELY.

11. The Corona virus probably means weddings, funerals, graduations, reunions, etc. will be limited to small gatherings of 10 or less or by video. Also probably no visits to hospitals, nursing homes, and no family gatherings, no church events, etc. until further notice.

12. Any service people, cleaning people, etc., coming to the house must stay 6 feet away, and hopefully they wear gloves.

13. Inconvenience is better than Illness.

14.

+++++++++++++++++++++++++

11. <u>SAVORING</u> By Donnie Powell 2/2020 (True)

I'm savoring the way we dance --Hold hands when we walk---Watch birds at the lake—Watch the way the wind and waves dance and sparkle at the lake—Watch the beauty of spring greening.

I'm savoring the way you take care of your friends and family--the way you laugh and your wonderful sense of humor.

I'm savoring the way you trust me more and more--maybe even totally--that's big.

I'm savoring the way you cook --I eat a lot at your house.

I'm savoring the way you double blink at me--sending me a double message maybe

I'm savoring your positive attitude, your uplifting view of life

I'm savoring the fun we have and the things we do and the places we go

I'm savoring the times you surprise me (Odyssey of the Mind, are you scared, chaired relay for life, etc.)

I'm savoring our little secrets (KEDN), a "Two dollar bill", "Sweet Kath-er-ine", supernova, top dog, picking up litter as we walk at the pond, 1-2 hours, dimples, she said "are you real" and while holding "I feel like this is where I belong"; earthquakes, "Sweet Vibrations", etc.

I'm savoring your boldness and your willingness to try new things.

I'm savoring your civic mindedness, volunteering, helping people, etc.

I'm savoring that you said you'd go steady with me.

I'm savoring how you helped me through (so far) the Covid-19 virus—we think alike. (4/2020)

I'm savoring that we nap in each other's arms awakening so entwined

I'm savoring that we hug and kiss and hold, yes hold—to hold is more than hug---hold is to bond. Hold is not so exciting but it's basic, it's foundational, it's innermost. I'm savoring to hold you.

I'm savoring our trips here and there and anywhere as long as I'm with you

I'm savoring you, you, you, you---who you are.

+++++++++++++++

#12. CARTOON-TOY MEMORIES BY RICHARD, SHARON, BEN June 2020 (True)

Note: I asked my children to list some of the cartoons/shows they remember watching when growing up and here are our emails. Brought back good memories.

+++

On Jun 21, 2020, at 1:47 PM, Donnie Powell <dd66rsb@cox.net> wrote:

Hello beloved,

Trying to remember what cartoons (or shows) Richard, Sharon and Ben watched Saturday mornings. The one day in the week we could sleep late was Saturday morning but yall were up early watching cartoons.   If I remember correctly, think some of them were (Oh we had only one TV)):

.1. Speed Racer

2. Lost World (Slee-stacks)

3. Ultra man   (Granny made Richard a costume of this man/creature that would raise his hand and say something (think it was "Ultraman" and transform into something--think it was called Ultraman.)

4.

5.

Later

A. Duck Tales (Ben said he learned a lot from this program)

B.

C.

Think Richard would dig thru his Leggos while watching tv.

++++++++++

Think the cartoons ended about noon????

Do yall ever think of trying to order them from ebay/Amazon and watching them again?

Love

Dad/O+PA

+++++++++++++++++

Sharon Hancock

<lafnspot@icloud.com>

6/29/2020 8:13 AM

To Richard Powell,   benjamin powell,   Dd66Rsb

Quick replyReply allForwardDelete

Being the middle child/only girl—I got to experience a wide variety of pop culture and general life experiences bc of my brothers—and the fact that our parents were very encouraging with everything we were interested in.

I watched all those with Ben too.
Didn't Ben have some rocks that turned into people, too or were those from Transformers that I'm thinking of?

Sharon Hancock

On Jun 29, 2020, at 8:04 AM, Sharon Hancock <lafnspot@icloud.com> wrote:

☐ YES! Wild Bill Hickock😊
He had hamster races. I wrote to them and they called me to be a guest. I picked the winning hamster (bc I have an eye for that sort of thing 😊)—I won a "My Little Pony" water park play set.
I don't remember Heckel and Jeckel though. Were they birds?
I remember one called Z-Force (I think)—-Richard liked them. They were like a Cartoon version of Power Rangers weren't they?

Sharon Hancock

On Jun 25, 2020, at 2:16 PM, Richard Powell <rchrd.powell@gmail.com> wrote:

☐
The new channel, bringing the total up to 5 was channel 46 which would play Mighty Mouse and Heckel and Jeckel weekday afternoons. It was hosted by some dude in a

cowboy costume(I think) and I believe Sharon was a call in guest one day.

On Jun 25, 2020, at 8:57 AM, Sharon Hancock <lafnspot@icloud.com> wrote:

☐ 1. Smurfs
2. Bugs Bunny etc
3. Care Bears (this may have been later with Ben)
4. Justice League
5. Snorks
6. Muppet Babies
7. There was one about animals with super powers (Of friendship and love☐) who lived in a tree.
8. Mighty Mouse
9. Hong Kong Fuey

Sharon Hancock
++++++++++++++++++++++++++
Yes! Rock Lords! they went along with GoBots. and also you mentioned Battlebeasts. other than the big main GI Joe, transformer big guns, Battle beasts were my favorite. they were just really cool. shame they didnt' catch on

On Thursday, June 25, 2020, 03:33:17 PM EDT, Donnie Powell <dd66rsb@cox.net> wrote:

Yes those are some more . Think there were some toys that looked like rocks but could change into a "person". And some little ones that didn't catch one too much that combined animals --thought they were clever.   Think He

man had a big tiger maybe.   Too bad we didn't keep all those toys ha ha.
Thanks for the memories.

Love Dad

On June 25, 2020 at 3:19 PM benjamin powell <lucidinkjunkie@yahoo.com> wrote:

I don't necessarily remember actually watching the cartoons on saturday morning. however, i've seen enough videos on youtube to know that the toys i played with were a direct result of the cartoons i saw - that was their marketing..... so lumping toys/cartoons together:
-transformers
-voltron
-g.i. joe
-thundercats
-he-man
-M.A.S.K.
-visionaries
-dino-riders
-teenage mutant ninja turtles
-challenge of the gobots

i also remember toys from:
-silverhawks
-inhumanoids
-centurians
-insectaurs
-jayce and the wheeled warriors(only found the name due to the youtube channel below.....)

the channel on youtube, toygalaxy, is really awesome. they address certain toys from various eras, with some really great commentary on various toys from that time. they cover both cartoons, and toys. they talk about how certain franchises got started, the peaks of some, why some failed, etc.

ducktales, chip n' dale rescue ranger, talespin, darkwing duck, gummy bears, stunt dawgs, SWAT kats all were in the 90s. biker mice from mars was from around that time too, though i remember the game more than the cartoon.

looking back, i watched some strange stuff as a kid
On Thursday, June 25, 2020, 02:19:15 PM EDT, Dd66Rsb <dd66rsb@cox.net> wrote:
I had forgotten quite a few. Thanks. Dad
On Jun 25, 2020 at 2:17 PM, < Richard Powell> wrote:
The new channel, bringing the total up to 5 was channel 46 which would play Mighty Mouse and Heckel and Jeckel weekday afternoons. It was hosted by some dude in a cowboy costume(I think) and I believe Sharon was a call in guest one day.

On Jun 25, 2020, at 8:57 AM, Sharon Hancock <lafnspot@icloud.com> wrote:
1. Smurfs
2. Bugs Bunny etc
3. Care Bears (this may have been later with Ben)
4. Justice League
5. Snorks
6. Muppet Babies
7. There was one about animals with super powers (Of friendship and love☐) who lived in a tree.
8. Mighty Mouse
9. Hong Kong Fuey

Sharon Hancock

+++

#13 SINGING AND DANCING IN THE SUNSHINE
(fiction) By Donnie Powell 3/28/2020

As we walked inside from the park, my wife asked if we had a good time

Our son answered. "Oh yes! I saw a rainbow, redbirds and some geese, and flowers everywhere, and I was skipping and laughing all morning while I was dancing and singing in the sunshine; and daddy was on the cellphone."

That's the first time I'd heard him all day and I said "I've got to go".

I hung up my cell and rushed to my bedroom as tears began to flow

I'd been given God's most precious gift of a child and time to spend with him

 and I had traded it for a bowl of porridge just as in the Old Testament

I'd always thought I had years and years with him but I knew in a twinkling he'd be grown

Now, I hoped he'd have happy memories so I knocked on his door and said lets go back to the park. We took his mom and we spent the day laughing and making memories as we were

SINGING AND DANCING IN THE SUNSHINE.

Yes we were singing and dancing in the sunshine all the years till he was grown.

+++++++++++++++

(Note: I enjoyed being a father to three wonderful children. As a gift one Christmas, I asked them to write some childhood memories. They did, and though none were of us singing and dancing in the sunshine, they were of happy childhoods. Thank you God for your most wonderful earthly gifts.)

++++++++++++++++++

#14. **<u>WAS AARON OLDER THAN MOSES</u>?**   (True) APR 2020

I asked in Sunday school of my teacher Bob Saint (?) was Aaron older or younger than Moses since he was not killed when the baby boys were killed in Egypt. No one knew. But next Sunday Mr. Arthur Boyette read the Bible and found the answer. Aaron was older. Exodus 7:7. (I cheated used electronics to help me.)

Mr. Boyette, the Postmaster there in Buena Vista told us to get our parents' approval. When I was in elementary school, we could buy Savings Bond stamps—the red ones were 10 cents and the blue or green ones were 25 cents. We pasted the stamps in a folder or bond and when full it was worth $18.75 or $18 something and if we held it for 7 years till maturity it was worth $25. I tried to cash mine to get the $18 there at the post office but Mr. Boyette had other ideas. Don't think I ever got my parents' approval. Not sure I ever cashed that bond.

+++++++++++++++

#15. ROCKING HORSE WITH RUNNING BOARD
(True) Apr 2020

When Richard was little, Santa brought a tall rocking horse that was too big for him to climb onto. Its design was such that there were two metal pipes as part of the support and to serve as stirrups on each side. So with a bit of effort, I fashioned a board between the metal on one or both sides which made it easier for Richard to climb aboard and helped him to stay aboard with his foot on it when he road and bounced up and down. Perhaps the only rocking horse with a running board in Georgia. Think we kept it and the running board for Sharon to ride since she is four years younger.

+++++++++++++

When Richard (or was it Ben) got a little yellow electric car, he couldn't reach the pedal. So devised a little box onto the pedal so he could reach it. He rode it all over the house. Might have had to add rubber bands to the wheels to get traction on the carpet.

+++++++++

When my grand-darlings came along I enjoyed getting them things like too many stuffed animals (which I think led to my giving stuffed animals away with a tag saying "…do a good deed …pass on or keep"… have given several thousand away with lots of blessings.). Managed to get used "green machines" pedal rides and they really loved them for several years—even put a car tag on one or both. To cut down on noise, put duct tape on tires. Even put a basket/box on one or both. Also bought a little red metal car frame for them to pedal—wooden training bike (that their cousin later rode around his house even late at night)—musical instruments (harp, accordions, xylophone, etc.,) dolls, etc.

+++++++++++++++++++++++++++++++++

#16. FROM WHENCE COMES THE SOUL—AND WHEN? ++ **And Other** ++April 2020

These are simple rhetorical questions (perhaps) with my thoughts added.

!st. Where does our soul come from (or from whence comes our soul?). My answer is from heaven, from God. The Bible says God made us in His image. To me that means He gave us a soul and maybe He gave us the ability to love. Imagine what human life would be without the ability to love. Thank you Lord.

2nd. And when do we get our soul? At conception? At birth? At the age we realize there is a God?   My answer is at conception.   But this leads to another rhetorical question.

2nd A. Delores and I had two miscarriages. If the soul comes at conception, will those two un-named babies know us in heaven?

++++++++++++++++++++

Jesus uplifted women. Had a woman (for example, Mary Magdalene) betrayed Him instead of Judas, women probably would have suffered for generations.

++++++++++++++

THE EARLY BIRD wants to be the first to Praise God.
(My thought Aug 2020)

++++++++++++++++++++

#17. A MILL JOB—DESPERATION TO ELATION -- May 2020 (fiction)

 "I'm with the local television station, interviewing people who have lost their job. The preacher told me you lost your job, would you tell me about your situation?"

"It's horrible. I had a job. I worked 12 hours a day, 6 days a week, sometimes 7 days. Then I was laid off. My wife is expecting a baby. We are homeless—living in the street. I have looked for work everywhere—there are no jobs—a few hours here or there. I swept out a barn yesterday, cleaned out a sewer last week, worked two days, the week before on a roofing job—barely enough to buy food. It breaks my heart that I cannot take care of my wife. We have gotten some help from the government, churches, family, and friends but they are strained too. I want to work. I want a job. If you have a job, thank the Lord and work extra hard to keep it.   The baby—our first born--is due in a week or two and we have decided we must give our baby up for adoption. It breaks my wife's heart but we have no choice. I—I cannot talk any more……"   That night they stayed at the local church and the pastor had been helping them with a number of things including an adoption agency.

Early the next morning, there was knocking at the church door. A man gave the preacher a written message and address. After a quick breakfast he loaded them into his car and drove them into a nearby town explaining that he thought the somewhat confusing message meant for them to meet the family that would be adopting their child—he had their address. As they drove down the street, they were impressed that the houses were neat and clean, even sidewalks, and backyards where the family could enjoy many activities and meet their neighbors and ….. tears dripped from the eyes of the parents-to-be. At the address they got out and looked around. A neighbor said hello and told how much he liked working at the mill, only worked 10 hours a day 6 days a week, with some holidays with pay, also sick days, and saving and retirement pay and just a great place to work. They walked up the sidewalk to the front door and knocked just as a mill representative arrived introducing himself and leading them inside. After a bit of confused talk the preacher said the message was not clear that he thought they were meeting the family who was adopting their child.

The mill representative apologized and explained that the mill manager had seen them on television, thought he would be a great worker at the mill. Told him he had a job at the mill. Said he sent a message to come to this address because with the job at the mill he had this house as long as he worked at the mill. Gave him an advance on his first paycheck. Explained there were groceries in the kitchen, and the house was furnished, and there was a store just down the street or they could shop in town. He gave them a list of phone numbers especially the hospital since she was nearing delivery time. He offered to give them a tour of the area and the town at their convenience. He gave them his number and said call anytime day or night. "We are family here. Welcome to the family." He left as they collapsed into each other's arms crying, praying, and laughing in disbelief.

(End—or a new beginning.)

Epilog: He was one of the hardest workers and most loyal. In a short time, he was promoted and always sang the praises of the mill and the mill family. His wife became a friend and leader among the mill wives and helped organize many charity events to help the less fortunate, especially the unemployed and homeless.

++++++++++++++++++++++++++

(Note: One of my now favorite series is "Call the Midwife". After watching all the series (some more than once) and hearing about unemployment due to Covid-19, had a dream about a couple expecting a child, I think in England, but he is unable to find a job and they must give baby up for adoption. Their situation is broadcast on tv and the owner of a worker-friendly mill in nearby town sees the broadcast and sends someone to bring them to mill-owned house and give him a job. They think they are going to meet people adopting their child. Thrilled when they learn he has a job and the house is theirs as long as he works there.)

++++++++++++++++++++++++++

#18 YAHWEH'S SONG BIRD May 2020 (fiction)

Mary and Joseph snuggled close together to try to keep warm on the cold, hard ground. Their journey to Bethlehem was slowed by her pregnancy and the hills were steep and the paths rugged. They were tired and the others nearby were all unhappy about having to stop their lives, make this difficult trip at the whim of Caesar. Everyone had to stop what they were doing, leave their families, their businesses, their crops, their animals, their homes, everything and go to be counted and bring money to be taxed—oh yes Caesar wanted taxes.

Joseph apologized for not bringing more blankets as he tried to hold Mary close for warmth—just as Jesus kicked him showing that He too was still awake. Then in a nearby tree a bird started singing quite loudly and Jesus immediately settled down. The bird kept singing even after someone nearby shouted, "Shut up bird, I'm trying to sleep". That did it. Mary started laughing and then Joseph joined in and they laughed out loud for several minutes. The laughter released all the built-up tension and they were able to relax and get a good night's sleep, serenaded by the singing bird.

Next morning, someone nearby asked if they were laughing during the night and Mary said they were. She said she felt Yahweh had sent the bird to encourage them all on their journey to David's town, that great things were about to happen, that the Messiah was about to be born, and to take heart and rejoice and sing as the bird had done. As the group started their day's journey, some were singing, thanks to Yahweh's song bird.

End

(Note: With no air conditioning in the mid 1960's in dorms at Georgia Southern, a Mocking Bird loudly serenaded us at about 300 am and one student yelled "Shut up bird I'm trying to sleep". Recently, heard a middle of the night Mocking Bird singing. Thought of Mary and Joseph sleeping on the cold ground and maybe they heard a bird in the middle of the night. From that came this story. Hope you enjoy.)

++++++++++++

#19. POND BANK   May 2020 (True)

At Walker's Pond in Warner Robins, a sign is posted listing the rules. One rule says they can fish only from the "pond bank". Overheard one man say, "we need to find the pond bank to get some fish." Cracked us up. (After circling the pond, I leaned out the window and told him he could fish from the shore line.)

+++++++++++++++

#20. MANKIND'S PHOENIX   May 2020 (Fiction)

(Note: Covid-19 and now riots in many cities resulted in this deathly story.)

In 2020, Covid-19 spread throughout the world with some religious leaders saying it was like a plague from God in old Egypt, a warning—perhaps a final warning. God wanted us to use the genius of man for peace and harmony—to work together—to make the planet a garden of Eden. But still the diverse camps continued working at odds—and Planet Eden fell far short of its intended purpose. And some religious leaders warned of rumbling thunder in the heavens.   Then in the USA came riots in many cities followed by more warnings from religious leaders. But sadly, Planet Eden got worse.

Sometime later, with amazing speed, a new virus swept the planet, with 70-90% death rate—everything changed—and the stench was terrible. Survivors' IQ was reduced to that of a child—barely able to feed themselves amidst the carnage, desolation, emptiness, and destruction. Infrastructure, transportation, growing crops, medicine, etc., all forms of civilization quickly collapsed. Almost overnight survivors returned to "cavemen era" living.

Their minds had been damaged so much that they could not remember many basic things such as reading. They could talk in simple terms only. Fortunately, the virus seemed to have gone away after a few weeks. Babies born after the virus left were mentally normal and their mothers retained instincts in how to birth and care for them as any wild animal does.

In a few years the children were able to see some old videos and books and learn to read and write. They banded together and began forming new schools. The children were mankind's rebirth.

Epilog: Before they died, some of the old religious leaders said the final virus was God's judgment for human's not listening to Him—He wanted humans to use their genius for good for peace, love, justice, kindness, working together, helping each other, etc. He warned us but we did not change. And now...............

End

++++++++++++++++++

#21. KALAHARI Jan 2018 By Donnie Powell

Epilog to movie "Sands of the Kalahari"

(This version changes the ending to the movie.)

As the rescue helicopter is waiting for OBrien (Stuart Whitman) to come join them, they realize he will not come because he will be facing murder charges. He would prefer to take his chances in the wild desert instead of the court room. Though he is probably a murderer, they wish to help him survive so they take things from the helicopter that he could use—blankets, canned food, tools such as an axe, shovel, a couple of knives, two pistols with 1000 rounds of ammunition, clothing, cans of fuel to burn for heat and cooking, tarpaulins, first aid kit, etc. They left him a note that they would return in a month to re-supply and he should leave written instructions to his company to set up a fund to reimburse them plus list any items he wanted on the following month's trip.

And so a re-supply system was put into place. Some argued that the police should go out and arrest him while others pointed out that he was in effect in prison—a self-imposed prison—and this was much cheaper than a trial and imprisonment. His company began working to have any potential charges dropped especially since the man he forced out of camp survived with the aborigines and was later found. The man that died, may have in fact died from the strain of the crash, hard living in the desert, etc. They thought the charges could be reduced to failing to report a death or manslaughter but under the unusual and unique circumstances they felt even those charges would be dropped. And so his lawyers set to work.

Meanwhile, OBrien continued in his survival mode. The extra ammo was greatly appreciated as he could now protect himself indefinitely against the apes. Despite earlier comments, he started eating them as one of the few sources of meat in the area. He was even able to capture one alive, tied her up, and denied her food and drink until she became less wild. He had tied her mouth mostly shut so she could eat but not bite him. She did not like her cage or being tied up but as the days went by, her hunger and thirst made her calm down. He liked having a companion and even talked to her and she learned the terms "food" and "water" and from there he was able to train her to "sit", etc.

He authorized his company to pay anything asked because he knew he needed the supplies. He asked for more long-range guns and ammunition and seeds to plant corn, beans, etc., near the water hole. A mattress was a welcome relief. He also asked for traps for the apes and other game. They even supplied him with salt, pepper, etc., plus more canned goods—and a can opener—enough for at least a year. He got some lumber with which he build a secure door, bunk, shelves, etc.   He also got chickens, hoping they could survive and not be eaten by local predators.   Though probably out of range, they provided him with a battery radio and a two-way radio so they could talk to each other when the supply copter came.

He encountered an aboriginal group and using sign language was able to trade for a "wife" or bed partner—he named her "Ug". She was beyond child bearing years with no surviving children and her husband had died—thus making her the ideal member for trade to OBrien. By American standards, Ug was not pretty at all, but in the dark she was what he wanted. At first she stoically accepted her fate and performed her duties solemnly. She worked hard at gathering what food she knew about—some she had to dig from the ground, other food she knew where to find—she also gathered fuel, cooked, and cleaned. After a few weeks she realized she was living better than she ever had—and with no men to look after her she would have been kicked out when food ran out, probably in the coming winter. She was amazed at the food from the cans and the dried/salted/preserved food in such abundance. With blankets, shoes, etc. she was warm and comfortable. With the realization, her attitude changed toward OBrien and she began to actively show affection and passion—which he liked. When she saw him kill a dominant male ape with his gun she was both terrified by the thunder of the gun and awe-struck by the long distance death and power held by her owner—she had never seen or heard such—she began to somewhat worship him and treat him as her lord and master. As she began to learn his language, she was able to ask what he wanted and was able to anticipate his every need.

He decided to build a small dam in the dry stream bed to catch and hopefully hold more rain water thinking that if it stayed year round maybe reeds and other plants would grow along its edge plus he could plant some crops nearby. Ug jumped in and helped him lug the rocks into place. Week after week it grew slightly but steadily. Ug explained their efforts to a visiting tribe who pitched in and helped (but secretly wondered why the white man would build a dam when they could just move on to where water was located). When the rains did come, the dam of course had some holes but did catch and hold water well enough that a small shallow lake was formed. In short order, birds and animals came there to drink which provided an additional food source. In time, fish and frogs appeared in the lake. Obrien thought perhaps birds brought the fish and frog eggs on their legs from other lakes. He did not know but they were welcome in his little "Lake Obrien".

Ug's tribe returned to visit and trade—he sort of established a trading post and other groups got the word and came to trade. As a result, his re-supply list began to include unusual things that his customers wanted. They had little to offer but he enjoyed the company and gave them good deals. Apparently Ug told them of his mighty power to create thunder and kill a big ape way beyond the range of their bows and arrows. They weren't sure they believed her but they did not want to incur his wrath to find out. One day as a tribe was visiting, a deadly snake slid into view—OBrien pulled his pistol and fired without thinking—all the tribe ran away screaming—except a couple who were too terrified to move. When OBrien held up the dead viper, the two remaining ones fell on their knees—he laughed and told Ug to have them get up—they could have the snake for skin and food which they gratefully accepted and hurried to catch up with their tribesman. After that when Ug told them something they believed her. They had trouble believing he could talk to a loud flying monster and command it to land and leave tribute of gifts. OBrien began to understand some of their language and suspected Ug was elaborating a bit—and surprisingly, since she slept with the "god" they began to respect and fear her a bit.

On her own, Ug thought to surprise her master with a gift of three younger women to sleep with him—to bear the children of the white god. She did this simply and easily and the three stayed behind when their tribesmen left—surprising OBrien—and happily having them cater to his every need and desire. Once they became pregnant they went back with their tribe on their next visit. Ug then made a similar arrangement with other tribes who were anxious to curry his favor and upgrade their descendants by mating with the thunder god. So in time, OBrien fathered numerous children some of whom came to visit and he recognized them immediately. Some of the women returned for a second round of mating. Also, the word spread to distant tribes who also brought their young women for impregnation by the white god.

During a visit by one tribe, Ug told them that the flying monster would come in a few days if they stayed nearby they could see and hear it and see how her master commanded tribute. Fearfully, they hid out and observed the helicopter land and leave gifts as OBrien stood nearby and directed it. With fear they fled and spread the word – they even drew pictures of the monster to show others. His legend spread and spread.

He was able to get each visiting tribe to tell him about their home ranges and he made a map of the area for hundreds of miles around. Only a couple had encountered a white man and a few went to trading posts run by Blacks. He got them to be on the lookout for certain valuable minerals—gold, diamonds, silver, etc. which they dutifully reported to him. With this information he realized there were some potential mining sites that could be very profitable. A surprising find was what he thought was an oil field—the topography plus samples indicated a possible large oil reserve.

One tribe told Ug they had found a white man in the desert and got him to a white settlement. Their description plus a crude drawing convinced Obrien that the man was the one he forced out of camp with the ostrich egg water bottles— he was secretly thrilled—he had not killed the man.

After quite a few years, Obrien's lawyers had good news and one came with a written offer of pardon if he came back and surrendered himself to authorities. He was delighted.

He spent the next hours deliberating his new option—would he be happier back in civilization or here in HIS domain where he was "lord and master" and every day was a challenge—where he felt alive. But there were so many luxuries back home—clean sheets, hot bath or shower, indoor plumbing, eating at restaurants etc. etc.,-- so many things he could do other than scramble for food all the time. If he left, he would leave his "kingdom" to Ug—but what would she do when the supplies ran out—she was tough, she would probably go back to her tribe. The lure of civilization as he knew it, was like a siren song and he—like Ulysses—felt its irresistible pull. But could he change from primal survival mode—he was not sure.

+++++++++++

What do YOU think he decided?

If he went back, wonder if he would try to have a reunion with the other crash survivors and try to make amends—bury the hatchet (not literally)--as best he could. Would they even speak to him?

 End

+++++++++++++++++

22. **JACOB'S AND JESUS' GARDEN**   (or "BLUE SKY MEANS YAHWEH LOVES US") .   June 2020--- (Fiction)

As a young boy, Jesus was working on His first garden when an older, homeless boy stopped and watched. They introduced themselves as Jesus explained what He was doing and invited Jacob to help, especially with removing a very large rock, which was barely doable when they worked together. Mary welcomed Jacob into their home and soon he was like a member of the family. Seemingly, in no time, the garden was flourishing. Jesus complimented Jacob for his special talent for growing things. They provided plenty of food for the home table and even sold some at the local market—a first for Jacob. They also gave some to widows and the poor. Jacob had found his calling—being a farmer.

Joseph recognized his talent and love of gardening and wrote a letter to a distant friend who had no children and no relatives but who had a farm. He responded quickly inviting (almost begging) Jacob to come live and work with him on his farm and if he was as good as Joseph had said, Jacob could begin buying parcels of his land each year. Jacob could not believe his ears—a permanent job and a permanent home and the possibility of owning land and a home. He, Jacob, a homeless orphan, a nobody might become a somebody because of his friend Jesus. (He could hardly swallow.)   He left for his new world the next day.

+++++++++++++++++++

Years later, Jesus and his disciples walked through Jacob's field.   They plucked   some handfuls of grain, rubbed/thrashed them to eat (which is considered work on the Sabbath) and the Pharisees saw this and criticized them for breaking the rules. Perhaps to reduce the tension, Jacob welcomed everyone to his home and offered them an already cooked meal. When no one was looking, Jacob smiled and winked at Jesus and began a discussion with the Pharisees.

Jacob: Learned and wise leaders, help me understand the scriptures which indicate the Messiah is to come lowly and to be tortured but also as our King and He is to set up a new kingdom. Some teachers say He is to come twice and others say there are to be two Messiahs. (He and Jesus smiled as they noticed the Pharisees squirming a bit because they were not prepared to answer such long-debated questions.) Your rules say it is blasphemy to claim to be the Messiah, the Son of God.

My question: When the Messiah comes, how will you know Him? If He follows your rules, He cannot tell you He is the Messiah. If He disobeys your rules, and tells you He is the Messiah, you will say blasphemy and punish Him. So when the Messiah comes, what is He to tell you?

Pharisees: He will perform miracles and signs.

Jacob: Such as healing the blind, the lepers, the lame? Feeding 5,000?

Pharisees: He will not do work on the Sabbath!

Jacob: So, He'd let someone go hungry or suffer all day on the Sabbath. The scripture says love the Lord with all your heart, mind, and soul. Would Yahweh want us to honor the Sabbath by letting someone suffer needlessly? Yahweh is The God of Love—He created earth for us—look at the blue sky and think of His love. He gave us brains to grow crops—He could have given us the brains of chickens but He loved us enough to give us brains to have dominion over all the earth—that's supreme love. When I lived with Jesus, His family showed me what love of family means and Yahweh's love is like that but so much more. He is a God of infinite, unfathomable Love not of rules where it is ok to help an animal while you let a human suffer. Yahweh sent John the Baptist who says the Messiah has come. Yahweh loves us enough to send a Messiah—we should know the Messiah and hear Him when He comes. If the

Messiah cannot tell you who He is when He comes, how will you know Him?

Pharisees: Uhhh, w-w-we will know Him.

Jacob: You have NOT known Him YET! Open your eyes! Open your minds! Who has already fulfilled the scriptures? Who has healed the sick right before your eyes? Who has worked miracles never seen before? Who preaches love and forgiveness? Who fed 5,000? Who is of the house and lineage of David? Who was born in the city of David? Who raised Lazarus from the dead? The Messiah HAS ALREADY COME! He is here today in THIS house! He is JESUS THE CHRIST! THE LIVING SON OF THE LIVING GOD! JESUS IS THE MESSIAH!

Pharisees: No, No. And they ran out.

But a couple knew in their heart of hearts that they had heard the truth—a great truth—the greatest truth—but would they have the courage to stand before the Scribes and Pharisees and testify to that truth in the synagogue?

After the Pharisees left, the disciples were stunned and speechless at Jacob's thunderous declaration of Jesus as the Messiah and Son of God. No one could argue with Jacob's logic and his persuasiveness.   And Jesus had not told him to be quiet.   Finally, Jesus, laughed and told Jacob if he wasn't such a good farmer He'd have him become a disciple. Then He had everyone gather around and told a parable of the Sewer, which Jesus said was inspired by Jacob sewing grain earlier in the year.

The next day as Jesus and his disciples were leaving, Jacob offered to follow but Jesus asked him to stay behind and to continue to grow crops, to send food/money/support from time to time and to always help the poor, homeless, and orphans which Jacob pledged to do. Jesus said with a smile, "Good farmers are hard to find—you feed their bodies, My disciples will feed their souls."

End

++++++++++++++++++++++++++++

Author's Note: A friend's son Jake has a luscious garden each year which got me to thinking about a young Jesus growing a garden. Of course He needed a friend to help whose name had to be Jacob. Their garden was to be the end but stories have a way of growing and the disciples threshing grain on the Sabbath came into the story. So Jake, thank you for having a garden.

++++++++++++++++++++++++++++++

#23. JESUS' SISTER SPEAKS (fiction) July 2020

"Mom, the other day when it started to rain, Jesus called us together and told us to watch the mother hen. We did and she called and gathered her baby chicks under her wings to protect them and keep them dry. We thought that was neat. We saw one that was late getting there and I asked if I should go pick it up and Jesus said 'No. the mother hen would think I was trying to hurt the chick and attack me pecking, scratching, and flapping her wings.' That would hurt wouldn't it Mom?' With a smile, Mary nodded.

"Mom, when we go on walks with Jesus, He teaches us many things. He even has us sit quietly until animals come close—sometimes close enough for us to pet them. Mom I petted a baby deer the other day—she was so soft—and then, poof she jumped away in a flash. Jesus is so calm and patient—all of our friends like being around Him. And He tells us stories of old—Noah, Moses, David and others. Mom, Jesus is my big brother but He is also a very special person, isn't He? "

Mary hugged her daughter and said, "Yes my darling daughter, you are special and Jesus is special in other ways to us and to everyone."

++++++++++++++++++++++++++++

+++++++++++++++++

27. JESUS SAID, "YES, IT IS YOU".   By Donnie Powell   Mar 2020 (Fiction)

(Note: Many times I've listened to the Statler Brothers sing a song where Jesus tells the Disciples that one of them will betray him and they ask "Lord, Is it I?" I began to think, what if I had been a disciple, maybe #13, and what if I asked that question. From that came this story.

"Lord Is It I?" by The Statler Brothers. –Lyrics--Even as great as He was There we those who wanted to kill Him And He knew it and told His disciples That He was going to be betrayed by one of the twelve.

They all sat down to share in a little room upstairs
The feast of the unleavened bread
Verily I say, one of you will betray
And the friends of Jesus answered and said
Lord, is it I? They all began to cry
Lord, is it I, is it I?

Will one of us betray, kiss and run away
Lord, is it I, is it I?
This bread is My body, this cup is My blood
This do in remembrance of Me
But after I go before the cock crows
Someone will deny knowing Me
Lord, is it I? They all began to cry
Lord, is it I, is it I?
Will one be ashamed to mention Your sweet name
Lord, is it I, is it I?
Lord, is it I, is it I?)
+++++++++++++

No one has ever heard of me and never will but here is my story. I lived a quiet average life but I was always afraid of the Romans, of my boss, the Scribes and the Pharisees and anyone in authority—some called me XX (your name maybe) the Scared One. Then one day, Jesus said, "Follow Me" and I dropped everything I was doing and followed Him. For once, I didn't stop to think, I just acted, and I am so glad I did.

Jesus taught us so much—Love God with all our heart and our neighbor as our self—Love and forgive—help others, and so much more. He performed miracles—I was there and I can still hardly believe what He did. He was—no is—truly the Son of God. I loved Him more and more every day.

I was in the boat when a storm came up. Jesus was so tired, He was asleep and we were all rowing and bailing and scared—but I was the most scared. Oh the wind was howling, the lightning and thunder, the waves were crashing—my teeth were chattering and my knees were knocking—oh I was scared. Finally, someone woke Jesus up and He said, "Peace. Be Still!" And it was. Not even a distant rumble of thunder. Not a whisper of wind. The sea was calm as glass. We all held our breath. Jesus smiled and said Were you afraid. I said yes, I even wet myself, but the storm was so bad nobody can tell. He smiled and said you weren't the only one.

Many times I was too afraid to try things but His faith and encouragement helped me to become a little less afraid and do some of the things the other disciples did.

When Jesus talked of His dying, I became very afraid. Once he even said one of us would betray Him. None of us believed that could happen, none but me. I asked him privately. "Lord, is it I?" I love You so much, but I know I am weak, please tell me if it is I who will betray you.

Jesus looked at me with a deep sadness in His eyes and said "Yes XX you will betray me. Yes, it is you." My heart broke and I fell on my knees weeping, begging him to give me strength not to do this terrible thing, to help me. I love you Jesus, I cannot betray you, I must not. Why, Why?

Jesus said, "It is My Father's plan, someone has to betray me so they can arrest me when the crowds are not around." But not me, I love you deeply. Jesus, I'll get on a ship today and go far away. I'll miss you sorely but that way I won't betray you. Please let me do that.

Jesus said, "If you do, then another disciple will betray me and your name will never be known as a disciple. History will never hear of you. Is that what you want?"

Yes, that is better than betraying you. Where ever I go, I will tell people about You and Your Good News. Jesus, my friend, the Messiah. Goodbye.

And I never saw Him again. But later I heard that Jesus was indeed betrayed, horribly crucified, and arose from the dead as He said He would. So let me tell you about this most wonderful Person in the world, my Friend, the Savior of all, Who loves you enough to die for you. Come let me tell you more about Him. One time there were 5,000 people and they were hungry and Jesus…

End

+++++++++++++++++++++

#28. JESUS TALKS TO JUDAS   (Fiction) June 2020 ((This is Not a happy story.))

(Dear Lord, help this story to be worthy.)

(Background: After hearing the Statler Brothers sing a song (see #27 above) "Lord Is It I" (about who will betray Jesus), this story/play/skit emerged. Also influenced by the first verse of their song "The King of Love".   The setting is a few days before the Disciples are to meet in the Upper Room. Jesus tells Judas someone is to betray Him. After Covid-19 ends, I want to present this live to my Sunday School Class ("The Becomers") with me playing the role of Judas and someone else reading the role of Jesus. Through the power of fiction,   my class members are to be magically teleported back in time and are to be part of the meeting with Judas perhaps pointing to some of them and saying "no, not xxxx to betray you Jesus". I hope to offend no one.) (In the skit, I'll play the role of Judas and will wear a costume so I can quickly remove the costume and return to myself.)

+++++++++++++++++++

"Lord Is It I?" by The Statler Brothers. (I'll try to play this song in class.)

("Even as great as He was, There we those who wanted to kill Him And He knew it and told His disciples That He was going to be betrayed by one of the twelve.)

They all sat down to share in a little room upstairs
The feast of the unleavened bread
Verily I say, one of you will betray
And the friends of Jesus answered and said
Lord, is it I? They all began to cry
Lord, is it I, is it I?
Will one of us betray, kiss and run away
Lord, is it I, is it I?
This bread is My body, this cup is My blood
This do in remembrance of Me
But after I go before the cock crows
Someone will deny knowing Me
Lord, is it I? They all began to cry
Lord, is it I, is it I?
Will one be ashamed to mention Your sweet name
Lord, is it I, is it I?
Lord, is it I, is it I?"
++++++++
"The King of Love" by the Statler Brothers. (I'll try to play the first verse of this song.)
Jesus said, "It has to be
The Father planned My destiny
This is My blood which I must give
I will die, so you may live"

He was a Child, He was a son
He was a Man among men

He was a Friend, He was a saint
He was the King of Love

Jesus died the world was dark
Not a sound was there to hark
The breath was gone, He hung His head
But wait, let us rejoice

For He has risen from the dead
He was a Child, He was a Son
He was a Man among men
He was a Friend, He was a Saint
He was the King of Love
++++++++++++++++

JESUS TALKS TO JUDAS.

JESUS: Judas, I want to tell you plainly, in a few days, I will be crucified. They are afraid of the crowds by day, so someone close to Me, will betray Me and lead them to Me at night.

JUDAS: NO. Jesus please say it is not so. Crucifixion is the most painful, horrible torture—no normal man would volunteer for that. You truly are the Son of God. You are the Messiah.

We must save you. If You know what they are plotting, come let us tell the others. We have time to leave the city. Come let us hurry.

JESUS: It is my Father's plan. I must be sacrificed for the sins of the world.

JUDAS: Isn't there some other way? Surely it can wait a few years. We can leave the city and continue to spread the

Good News. You can send us out again two by two—oh Jesus remember how wonderful that was—with Your power, I, even I, with these hands, these hands healed people in Your name. I remember a little blind girl—the first person she ever saw was me. Let's go back, I'd like to see her again. And there are others waiting for You.

JESUS: The time has come.

JUDAS: Sir, please, the world needs You. Even a couple more years and the number we can heal and tell about God's Love. And …. And

JESUS: Someone will betray me.

JUDAS: Not one of the disciples! NO!

> Not PETER. You said Yourself he is our rock and he is our leader—sometimes we have to talk to him but no not Peter.

> Not JUDE. You have seen him with little children. He is so good with them. He wants to start a children's hospital where they can be treated free of charge…. No not Jude.

JESUS: Maybe it will be Mary Magdalene?

JUDAS: NO No No. Jesus she worships the ground You walk on. When You are around she never takes her eyes off you. Your ministry has lifted women to levels equal with men, if she or any woman betrayed You, it would set women back hundreds and hundreds of years. But Mary could never, ever betray you. No, not Mary.

JESUS: Then who?

JUDAS: (Look at a member of the SS class, call their name

No, not Karen, she has been faithful all her life—why even in the womb she heard preaching and was called and became a follower, a teacher, a singer, a witness, …No not Karen.

No, not Brad, he works in the food pantry and helps the hungry as You have commanded, and he helps Celebrate Recovery,…. No Not Brad…………….

No, not Maxine, her happy laughter, she has devoted her beautiful voice to You all her life, singing countless songs of praise, her heart would break at the thought of betraying You.

No, not ___________

JESUS: Then who?

JUDAS: Not the Sons of Thunder—they are so close to you they are always right there with you, they are so loyal, no not them………

JUDAS: Not MATTHEW—he is writing down Your miracles and teachings. I have read some of what he has written and there is so much love and devotion and ….no not Matthew.

JUDAS: Not Philip…. Not any of the other disciples--- they have given up everything—they love You totally--- they will follow You the rest of their lives---No not any of the disciples………….

JESUS: Judas—it is you—you are the one to betray me.

JUDAS: No, dear Jesus no, please. Please, let's leave town, avoid the crucifixion, send us out again. Please I don't want to betray you.

JESUS: You have gone down the list. There is no one else. It has to be. My mission is to be sacrificed. You are to betray me. It is you.

JUDAS: No please no.

JESUS: Go and do what you must. Make arrangements. Go now. And Judas, there will be some money in it for you.

JUDAS: What? Money! Did you say money? I-I'll go. (Mumbles: I wonder how much I can get.) ((Departs, as the devil enters him.))

(End)

++++++++++++++

#29. <u>YOUNG JESUS WASHES FEET</u> (Fiction) June 2020

Joseph was out of town when three armed, dirty men burst into their house demanding food and money. Mary and young Jesus took protective stances between them and the children. After a few moments of silence, Mary quietly but commandingly said. "This is a house of peace, put your weapons away and clean up while I prepare food for you." They were accustomed to people being frightened into obedience not calmly giving orders, which they quickly followed. When they sat down, Mary thanked Yahweh for the meal before allowing the visitors to eat—another first.

During the meal, Jesus took a basin and towel, knelt, and washed each man's feet and cleaned their sandals—after which each man fell silent—deep in thought.

As they started to leave, Mary handed them some food to take with them. Jesus looked each in the eye and said, "You are now ready for the change that is coming."

They traveled a short distance, sat down and just thought in silence. After some time, each took out their weapons and tossed them behind some rocks, and then went on their way.

They came upon some men about to have a meal and were invited to join. They shared the food Mary had prepared and surprisingly it was enough for everyone. As they ate and talked, two of the men were looking for workers to become fishermen, one was a salesman, and several were officers of the law looking for armed, hardened criminals heading in their direction. The lead officer asked the three to tell about themselves.

The leader of the criminals told of bursting into Mary's house but when he saw her, he thought of a mother bear protecting her young and caught his breath. Then when he looked at her Son—named Jesus—he thought about Isiah calling down fire from heaven* and he stepped back. "But Mary told us to put aside our weapons and clean up and she fed us. While we ate, this Young Boy—this Prophet— washed our feet—and, and…it was like, like He washed my soul, clean and pure of all the bad things I had ever done. Tears came to my eyes for the first time in years. I was so overcome I could not speak until just now. It was a holy moment. (After a deep breath)   We are the guilty ones you are looking for—do with us what you will. The Young Prophet told us as we left—'You are now ready for the change that is coming.' I am ready."

The other two said they were ready also.

After a long silence, the lead officer said at first he thought the three were the ones but they were not armed and criminals didn't take time to clean up especially time to wash their feet and sandals, plus they didn't have that hardened look in their eyes. "I think those hardened criminals no longer exist—I think they have encountered a Young Prophet—maybe a Messiah—Who has changed their lives forever by washing their feet."

End.

Epilog: The three former criminals went with the two men who were looking for workers and became fishermen.

*2 Kings 1:10

+++++++++++++++++++++++++++

#30. YOUNG JESUS VISITS DEAD POND.   (Fiction) July 2020

The drought and famine were terrible and food was scare but fortunately their garden continued to produce. Joseph had little work and decided to go to the nearest large town seeking work while asking Jesus and James to go hunting and fishing in hopes of finding food. Through the years, Joseph had carved beautiful manger scene figures honoring Jesus' birth. Jesus brought them to Joseph asking him to try to sell them to buy food. At first Joseph objected but Jesus said he could carve more when he returned.

Jesus asked Mary for her outside pot in which to cook fish soup and also some of her special seasonings. When He told her they were going all the way to Dead Pond, Mary said, "But Jesus, Honey, there are no fish there, that's why it is called Dead Pond, you won't…uh ....I'll get what You need to cook Your fish."

After she left, James said, "She calls me honey too." Jesus smiled and said, "She called Me her Baby until you came along. But I like hearing her call me Honey. She is the only one who will ever call Me that. Now let's get everything ready so we can leave early tomorrow."

Next day, after a few hours of travel, James asked, "What is Your hurry?" A few minutes later, they rested at a small stream when their cousin John rushed up saying, "Hurry, come on." And they were off. A few hours later they arrived at Dead Pond to find several starving families fishing with no success. John rushed up to one family with a small baby and gave them some wild honey that he had gathered—even the baby was able to eat some watered down honey, which revived her just in time. He shared the remainder of his honey with each of the other families. As they gathered around, Jesus introduced Himself, His brother and then their cousin John saying one day he will be called John the Baptist, a prophet. That statement surprised everyone including James and especially John. Jesus showed them His pot saying for each of them to toss their line in the water, they would catch a fish for each member of the family plus one more which they were to clean and bring to Him for the cooking pot.

One said, "We have been fishing for days and caught nothing".

John took his pole and said, "But now JESUS is here. Come let us do what He says." And they were off in a mad dash. If a future prophet was willing to fish in a dead pond when commanded by a young Boy Who spoke with authority, then maybe, just maybe they would have fish to eat today—ummm, fish.

James was stunned and speechless for a bit. Finally, he asked Jesus, "Should I get wood for the fire or go fish?"

Jesus smiled, and said, "I'll get the wood. Don't you want to be able to say you caught a fish from the Dead Pond?" James whooped and was off like a shot.

After eating their fill, there was laughter and friendly talk and finally someone asked Jesus how He knew there would be fish, if He too was a prophet, if He knew when the drought would end, if they stayed by Dead Pond would they be able to continue catching fish, and many more questions.

Jesus said He knew Yahweh would provide. That God loves all his children. Then Jesus spoke to them about the scriptures and explained what they meant. "He said a couple of years ago, John and I traced the creek that feeds Dead Pond and found a place where the water from another creek was bad. We were able to dam that creek up and divert the water into the desert. And like Moses, we found a special tree * and threw it into Dead Pond and now the water has been cleaned up and Yahweh has sent the fish— God provided." He went on to say, that the drought was coming to an end and they could return to their homes. He told them to take some of the special fish soup and like Elijah and the widow's **   flour and oil, the soup would last their household and hungry friends until the drought ended.

The next morning, everyone left early with renewed faith and some of Jesus' soup to see them through the hard times. They would remember His teachings and were not surprised some years later to hear the name of John the Baptist and of course Jesus—and they followed.

Jesus, James, and John traveled together until John said his goodbyes. Jesus hugged him and told him some things in private and he was gone.

James kept looking at his Brother as they walked—not knowing what to think—how did He know about the fish. And the scriptures—they made so much sense now. And cousin John to be the Baptist and a prophet? He wondered—"Who is this my Brother"?

When they paused for lunch, James asked, "What is that You are crunching on?"

Jesus tossed him a couple saying, "Try them, they are good."

James crunched down and noticed they were cooked and dipped in honey, and commented, "They taste good, but what are they?"

Jesus said, "John's locusts."***

(End)

++++++++++++++++++++++++++++

(Note: Joseph had found work and had returned shortly before Jesus and James got home with some fish soup for supper. Joseph also had food and some money but had kept the original manger scene figures but had managed to sell new ones he had carved while away, thus supplementing his carpentry earnings. It was a good family homecoming.)

*Exodus 15: 26-27   ** 1 Kings 17: 16   *** Matt 3:4

++++++++++++++++++++++++++++++++++++

#31. YOUNG JESUS HEALS INJURED PUPPY (Fiction) July 2020

"Momma! The cart ran over my puppy and he's hurt!" wailed a tearful friend of Jesus' sister.

Her mother took the puppy, hugged her daughter and was saddened because she could not ease the suffering of her child. She said, "Oh Honey. I'm sorry, but your puppy is not just hurt he is……"

"No, No No!" groaned the weeping child as she grabbed her puppy and ran saying "My friend Jesus will fix my puppy and make him well."

Young Jesus was outside the shop using a drawing knife to shape a piece of wood when He heard His young friend yelling, "Jesus, Jesus Jesus!"   He lay aside His tools and knelt as she flew into His arms showing Him her pup and saying "He's hurt bad, please make him well."   Jesus looked into her trusting eyes and was moved with compassion—such faith He was not to see again for years.

He glanced up as Mary told the girl's mother, "Jesus' time has not yet come" and she said, "But my little girl's heart is broken and I'm helpless to do anything. But Jesus can." Then she looked at Jesus and clearly mouthed the word, "PLEASE".

Jesus hugged the girl, cleared His throat, stood and said, "Let me have the pup, maybe he just had the wind knocked out of him. Maybe you and my sister could say a prayer to Yahweh."

He took the pup and walked a short distance away, as the sincere, earnest prayers of Jesus' sister, Mary, the girl and her mother were all lifted to Yahweh. A few moments later, the girl was on her knees deep in prayer when she felt the warm tongue of her pup as he pounced on her knocking her to the ground as she squealed with delight saying over and over "Thank You Jesus, Thank You Jesus!"

The girl's mother also joined in hugging and thanking Him. Jesus said, "Your girl has a lot of faith, more than a mustard seed, enough to move mountains."

To which her mom replied, "And she knows in Whom to place that faith".

(End)

++++++++++++++++++++++++

Epilog: That night the girl slept peacefully with her puppy while her mother awaited her husband's arrival from work. When he arrived, she threw her arms around him crying and saying over and over, "I'm sorry, forgive me." He was shocked. Finally they sat and talked asd she explained what had happened with the puppy. She explained that since the death of their baby son, she had become bitter and angry at Jehovah, the world and her husband. Today her daughter's faith was so strong that even she believed Jesus could heal the puppy—which she knew was dead—not knocked out but dead. She told her husband, she wanted to spare her daughter the hurt of losing her puppy but she could not, but because of her daughter's overwhelming faith, for a moment she believed and mouthed the word to Jesus "Please". "And with that, my anger and bitterness melted away. If you will let me, I want us to be a real family again, I will do my share. Please." And so the mustard seed size faith of a child moved a mountain of anger, bitterness and hurt.

#32.   YOUNG JESUS AND JOHN GO TO GALILEE
(fiction) July 2020

As young men, Jesus and John took a trip to the Jordan River, Sea of Galilee, and Jerusalem areas. They talked to each other of their future plans and visited places that would become important in their missions. They visited in the synagogues, sometimes teaching and sharing—a few times John gave fiery sermons which were eye openers especially when he shouted "repent the Messiah has been born in the city of David in Bethlehem and His time is coming in my lifetime. The scriptures will be fulfilled." As two young men, they enjoyed hunting, fishing and camping along the Jordan with John saying he felt the Jordan would be a big part of his future mission and Jesus agreed saying this is where you will become known as John the Baptist because you will baptize people who repent and turn away from their sins—and when they are ready for their calling-- "now let's fish and then swim".

In Jerusalem, John felt a dark moment at Herod's castle and Jesus did at Golgotha. They looked knowingly at each other—nodded and went on their way. They spent a night in the Mount of Olives with much time in deep prayer, in the morning greatly renewed.

One morning at the Sea of Galilee, they waded in the water and Jesus smiled at the young fishermen, one about His age, others some older. They had not caught much but generously offer Jesus and John a meal that was already cooked on the fire. Jesus and John accepted an invitation to go fishing that night—a first for each—they loved it—in the company of rugged competent men helping (sometimes awkwardly) them do their work with great appreciation of how difficult it was—but doing it well enough to earn the fishermen's respect. At the end of the long back-breaking smelly night of work, they had a nice catch and everyone was pleased but the work was not done. Sort the fish, clean and cook some, sell some, clean and repair the nets, and finally breakfast of the caught fish. They had to learn how to cook them the Galilean way to make them taste just right. The fishermen invited them to stay and become fisherman by trade but Jesus declined with a smile saying He planned to be a different type of fisherman one day. John said he loved it but he must return to the desert to prepare for another calling in answer to Yahweh. The fishermen wished them well and bid them come see them again.

Before they left, a nearby fisherman came over saying his boat's helm had a crack and asked if anyone had ever bored two holes and driven in wooden spikes or dowels to mend it. He said he had the tools and repair wood but none of his crew had the carpentry skills. After everyone else said no, Jesus said He'd take a look, so they all went over to see if this Youngster knew carpentry. They looked at His hands and thought maybe. They had beached the boat and had it ready. Jesus tapped to be sure the helm was sound and it was. He clamped the helm to be sure it would remain not move. He measured, checked the tools, dowels, selected the correct size bit, began with the brace and bit, and slowly drilled a hole straight and true. Then He tapped the dowel all the way in, cutting off the excess. He did the same for the second hole and the helm was good and strong and ready for use. Jesus suggested they put it in the water so the dowels could absorb some water and be a perfect fit.

The fishermen thanked Him and suggested He open a carpentry shop nearby because He would have plenty of business. They knew competence and talent when they saw it and they liked each of these two young men. They knew what Jesus had done especially with the brace and bit took a lot of strength and were surprised at how strong He was.

Later word had spread that a carpenter was visiting and a local approached Jesus and invited Him to look at his wife's broken rocking chair that belonged to her grandmother. Before He left, a redheaded young fisherman asked Jesus to give a blue stone to the man's daughter but Jesus suggested he come give it to her himself to which he said he couldn't talk to girls. John accompanied Jesus and together they carefully examined the heirloom with John commenting on the type of wood and saying he had seen a seasoned one not far off the trail they had traveled and if he could borrow a saw, he'd go get a piece big enough for Jesus to replace the broken rocker. Jesus agreed. While John and the man went to get the saw, his grown daughter asked Jesus if John had a girlfriend back home. Jesus told her neither He nor John would ever marry because Jehovah had a different path for each of them to travel, He said John was the greatest man He would ever know, he was a prophet of the One True God and would lead many to repent but sadly as with so many prophets, he would be killed as a young man for preaching the truth and doing good.   Then He told her He had met a young redheaded fisherman who was interested in her, just as there was a knock on the door.

Jesus began preparing the chair so that when John returned, He quickly fashioned a new rocker out of the slim tree section John brought.   With careful, deliberate almost artistic precision, He prepared the new rocker so the angle would be perfect. When almost done, he used a piece of broken glass to smooth the wood and finally a smoothing stone to make the wood very smooth. Then using strong glue, pegs, careful precise fittings He repaired the chair good as new. After the glue dried, they painted it the color she wanted and when she sat in it, remembering rocking her babies, she shed some happy tears as she flew to Jesus and John giving them motherly hugs of appreciation and love. And just like that, each was ready to go home. They said their good byes and were on their way.

NOTE: Years later, Jesus visited the daughter's house as she rocked her baby in that very same rocking chair, she told Him as she did every visitor, how two young strangers repaired the chair for her mom some years ago. He was a great carpenter the chair never squeaked and the other was to be a prophet—I hope so—we need prophets teaching God's Word and doing good. Her husband suddenly snapped his fingers saying "Girl, He's the Carpenter. Don't you recognize that smile, that twinkle in His eyes, those strong, rugged, calloused hands, His voice—He fixed your mom's chair that you are rocking our baby in—it is Him! He's come back to us." Jesus smiled as He noticed the blue stone on the mantel.

Author's comment: My Granddad Powell had a blacksmith shop where he made among other things axe handles and had us scrape and smooth the handles with broken glass. My Dad often told jokes with a twinkle in his eyes. My Mom, my wife and I all enjoyed rocking our babies.

+++++++++++++++++++

#33. YOUNG JESUS AND JOHN—DESERT RESCUE
(fiction)   July 2020

Another time, Jesus and John were headed into the wilderness to pray and meditate when John said "Did you hear that?"

Jesus said, "My ears are not as keen and attuned to the wilderness as yours."

John said, "Someone is lost and in trouble. This far out they better be riding a camel."

Jesus laughed saying, "John, that's funny. Lead the way— let's rescue the lost souls."

After several minutes they came upon a young man and woman who had passed out. Jesus wondered how John heard them, because He never heard anything. They quickly moved them to the shade of some rocks and gave them some of their water.

After a few minutes they come to but were very weak. The man said, "I thought I knew a short cut but got a little lost and then completely turned around. Are we far from the road?"

John said, "Out here, a little lost is all it takes. You are a long way from the main trail. After you rest, it will take us several hours to get you back to safety. Jehovah was looking after you; especially since we thought about coming next week but decided to come today."

Jesus said, "It is your good fortune that John has such keen hearing, he heard your call for help, I did not hear anything."

The man said, "But we haven't had water in so long, we haven't made a sound in hours."

 John said, "Then I heard your spirit calling—your guardian angel called and I heard."

Jesus said, "He is not kidding—He is a prophet who hears Jehovah's angels."

John and Jesus escorted them all the way to their home and even visited a couple of nights becoming better acquainted with their desert friends Martha and Lazarus as well as their sister Mary.

++++++++++++++++++++++++++++

#34. YOUNG JESUS AND JOHN MEET TWO BLIND MEN   (fiction) July 2020

On their way to solitude in the wilderness, John said, ""We can take a rugged short cut just past a stream around the next bend. We will have to crawl on our hands and knees part of the way and maybe use our ropes but it will save us some time and it will be fun. "

Jesus commented, "You know your way around this desert better than I do and going with you is always an adventure."

As they approached the stream, they saw two men, who called out when they heard someone approaching. "Help us. We are blind. The man leading us to the next town deserted us and we are stranded and everyone that has come by refused to help us. We are hungry and lost. Please lead us to the next town so we can beg for food."

Jesus and John gave them some of their food and examined their eyes while asking them if they had any family, how long they had been blind, what they did before they lost their eyesight, and generally getting to know them. Each had been skilled and made a good living until they could no longer see which led to their families leaving them and them becoming beggars on the street.

Jesus and John got some mud from the stream and put it on the eyes of the blind men while telling them not to wash it off until it had dried and explaining that they would not lead them to the next town. However, when they washed the dried mud off, their eyes would be soothed and things would be much better.

Jesus said, "John is a prophet and when he says things will be better, then they will be."

John told them, "The Messiah has been born. He will be known to all in my lifetime. The Messiah is coming to change everyone's heart!"

One blind man asked, "Are you the Messiah?"

John replied, "No I am not."

The other blind man asked, "Is your friend the Messiah?"

John was silent as he and Jesus left.

The blind men were doubly excited. Two young men had given them food, put mud on their eyes, given them hope that things would be better, and those men were a prophet and probably the Messiah—yes THE Messiah. No one would believe them. They'd just think they were two blind men wanting attention and handouts. But they knew—they would always know—they had talked to a prophet named John and THE Messiah whose name they failed to get.

Then they remembered the mud—it was dry. Hastily they stepped to the stream and washed and washed it off until it was all gone and and and….each could see.

"Look! What color is that bird? It's red! What color is that flower? It's yellow! Look at Yahweh's blue blue sky!" They hugged and shouted and jumped in the stream like rambunctious children (probably causing the angels to smile). Their joyous shouts of I CAN SEE! I CAN SEE! I CAN SEE! Echoed throughout the trail along with their laughter until they fell down exhausted.

One said, "This must be what it feels like to be born again."

The other said, "Yes. Come let's go tell the world we were healed by a young prophet and the long awaited Messiah and to repent and get ready because the young prophet said in his life time the Messiah was coming to change our hearts. They must believe us because we are no longer blind—they cannot argue with that fact. So the Messiah IS coming. Praise God."

(End)

++
+

+++++++++++++++

#35. YOUNG JESUS AND JOHN DIG A WELL (Fiction) July 2020

As they walked in the wilderness, Young Jesus said, "This is a lot farther than we have ever gone before."

John: "I've found a new campsite, a little cave, I think you will like it. I plan to stay there quite a bit."

Jesus: How did you find it?

John: I spend a lot of time out here. Remember our cousin who used a forked limb off a tree to try to find water? On an earlier trip, I used a forked limb and found a spot that may have water. Say, how did Jacob know where to dig a well? How did he know there was water at that spot? "

Jesus: "Good question. I don't know. What do you think?

John: "Near the camp, there is a place that looks very similar to the area around Jacob's well--the slope of the land, the shrubs, and the rock formations. That's where the forked stick indicated there is water down below. If we dug a well, we could stay longer. I could even live out here."

Jesus: "What's this WE? Me? Dig a well—I'm a carpenter. And you want to live out here?"

John: I already have shovels, a pick axe, ropes, buckets, everything we need. We could start today.

Later that night, John told Jesus that more and more he felt compelled to seek the solitude of the wilderness—to spend time in prayer and meditation. Jesus nodded, adding that they needed much prayer time and understanding of their future missions.

John: One day, if I have disciples, I may bring them here for a retreat—for a time of prayer and dedication to Jehovah—away from all outside distractions. So, let's get an early start on digging that well deeper tomorrow.

A couple of days later they did find water and they jumped up and down shouting in excitement like two little boys. But then finding water in the desert is something to get excited about.

John: That is the best tasting water I have ever had. Maybe it tastes so good because we worked so hard for it.

Jesus: I hereby name this "John's Well."

John: Thank you. I now have a greater appreciation for all well diggers. Jesus nodded.

That night, John said, "There are several places that could benefit from a well, if there is water in the area." He and Jesus listed several. Then discussed how to secretly buy the land and quietly dig the well—sometimes at night--and turn it over to the local synagogue.

Jesus asked, "But what if we dig the well and there is no water?"

John said," Then the local synagogue will be the proud owner of a deep, dry hole in the ground."

Jesus went outside just before dawn the next morning to get some fresh water and came back and woke John up laughing and saying, "John come outside and see what's at your well."

John sleepily went outside and stopped in his tracks; then they both burst out laughing. There by the well stood a camel obviously wanting some water. So they got the rope and bucket and started drawing water for their thirsty visitor. They found a hollowed out spot in a big rock that made a good trough. So they made sure to keep the trough filled.

Later John said, "I've never ridden a camel, let's take turns and see if we can ride without falling off. And they did—with lots of laughter and no falls. When they returned they took their animal friend with them because the owner would be looking for it—and besides, that was the only time they could ride out of the wilderness.

Over the next couple of years, they were able to dig a few wells each of which produced good- tasting water for many years. In time, small villages did spring up around the wells but no one ever knew who dug the wells. The locals said they were a gift from Jehovah and His angels.

After they dug the last well, John told Jesus, "If the wells survive, eventually, grass, flowers, and bushes will grow and perhaps a village may spring up at each well—right in the middle of nowhere. I just realized this--You, the Messiah, are like water in the desert---water brings physical life—You bring eternal life. Our time draws closer—we will be ready."

(End)

Note: My Grand Dad Powell was supposed to be able to find water using a Y shaped tree limb (peach?).

+++++++++++++++++++++++

<u>#36 YOUNG JESUS AND JOHN--BOAT RESUCE (Fiction) July 2020</u>

As young Jesus and John hiked along the Sea of Galilee, they came upon a clear spot with a small stream that was ideal for their night time camp. They set up a camp area including getting wood ready for a quick fire start, set their ground cloths and blankets aside, cleared an area, and went to the shore line to fish for supper. They tossed their lines in the water, cleaned up, looked at each other and laughed, commenting that their ropes and knives were just part of their bodies because they didn't leave them in camp. Jesus saw a warped board and commented that he could use it in the shop back home and asked John if he would like to help carry it back. John declined saying, "It would be best used as a cover for a chicken coop. Or a little boat for kids to play with." They laughed at the possibilities.

 As they relaxed and waited for a bite they noticed a boat with passengers passing fairly close to shore. They knew it was a ferry type boat that took people from one side of the Sea to the other for a fee. As it drew nearer, they simultaneously jumped up waving their arms and shouting, "You are sinking! Look out!"

They ripped off their shoes and outer clothes, kept their knives, tied a rope to the warped board and the other rope to a nearby short log and rushed into the water toward the sinking boat. As they got closer, they heard cries of "I can't swim! Help! Save me!" Just as they got close one woman fell in with her baby, she lost hold of the baby who sank but John dove down and came up with the screaming infant and placed it on the warped board which now became a little life boat. Jesus steered the mother to the board, telling her to kick her feet to stay afloat which she did—she somehow trusted His calming voice. John went aboard and began ripping out boat parts and tying them together as a small raft for people to hold onto to stay afloat. When he steered then to the makeshift raft their panic left them.

Jesus saw a woman desperately trying to keep her head and her baby's head above water. As He swam closer He realized she was trapped. He dove down and saw her leg was tangled in the ropes. He used His knife and after three dives freed her, but she had lost her baby. Jesus dove down and brought the crying baby up to a crying mother and steered them to the warped board.

Jesus dove after a man who took his bag, jumped overboard and sunk like a rock. Jesus tied His end of the rope to the bag, grabbed the man and dragged him to the surface where he coughed and sputtered saying "my bag, my money". Jesus handed him the rope and moved on to help others as one woman said, "He's a young tax collector, why didn't you let him drown?"

Finally, they had everyone holding onto something and reasonably calm. They explained that they would help take the women and children and swimmers to shore first, start a fire and use their dry blankets to warm them up. They asked the boat owner to stay with any non-swimmers and the swimmers to use some boards to be sure they stayed afloat that the swim was longer and tougher than it looked. When they reached shore, they would ask for one volunteer to go north and one to go south to get help for the women and some boats to come help tow the boat ashore.

Once the women were warm ashore, they would come back for the non-swimmers. They would not leave them on the water over night.

And that's what happened. Everyone was saved—cold, frightened, hungry but safe and very thankful to two young quick-witted strong capable men who put their lives in danger to help others. Their commanding voices and presences saved the day. (and the tax money.)

(End)

Note: Their fish lines had caught large fish which they cooked and shared with all the hungry survivors and those who came to help them. The terror, the panic, the cold water, finally firm ground, the warm fire, the food, exhaustion, the release, the blankets, sleep. Next morning—they could not thank Jesus and John enough—names they would praise and remember for years.

++++++++++++++++++++++++++++++++++++

#37. YOUNG JESUS AND JOHN---LOST BOYS (Fiction) July 2020

Young Jesus and John were visiting some cousins who lived near the Jordan River for a few days when a neighbor burst in asking if her boys were there. They had gone to the river with some other boys but had not come back for supper and they were nowhere to be found in the village and the mother broke down into tears.

An impromptu meeting happened immediately in the center of the village with everyone talking at once and nobody doing anything, until Jesus called for quiet. He asked a number of pertinent questions of the boys they were with after assuring them they were not in any trouble. The first question was did they cross the Jordan—after a moment of hesitation they nodded yes as their parents yelled "You know you're not supposed…" but stopped when Jesus raised a quieting hand. Jesus asked if they were looking to steal some melons or go swimming or go to a secret cave and so on. He asked the mother what they were wearing, type of sandals and if there were any special marks on the sandals to which one of the boys said one of the sandals had a "V" carved in it by the boy to be sure everyone knew it was his. Jesus asked if they had food and had they ever run away and a few other questions. Then Jesus organized search parties into groups of 2 or 3 with torches, blankets, food and water and told them to follow Him and the boys to where they were last seen so that John could look around. John was a great outdoorsman and could find tracks and clues that few others would see.

When they arrived at the river, Jesus had them stop and be quiet while John questioned the boys and then by torch followed the tracks until they were obliterated by other steps. Then he circled in wider and wider loops until he finally found a trail the "V" sandal cinched it. He followed it until he was satisfied and then he motioned everyone to follow by spreading out. They hadn't gone very far before it was obvious that the boys had become lost and had gone in circles and then went not toward the river but away from it. Then John and Jesus told everyone to be quiet and they shouted the boys' names. Silence. Again. Silence. Then the villagers moved forward again behind Jesus with John tracking the erratic wanderers. After a few minutes they stopped and shouted—silence. Move—stop—shout—silence. On and on into the night. John commented that at least they had not panicked and just run until exhausted—but they should be tired and stopping to rest soon. Move—stop—shout-silence. Move-stop-shout-silence. Again—move--stop—shout—someone on the left heard an answer. Everyone held their breath as the man on the left shouted and they all heard a weak but definite answer. The entire line began to move in that direction carefully, lest they bypass the boys in the dark. The villager kept calling and the answer kept getting closer and closer until finally the villagers found them huddled together shivering. Their dad quickly wrapped them in a blanket as neighbors gave them water and food and helped bundle them up. One son said, "Who moved the Jordan?" Which brought laughter, breaking the tension. The other son asked, "Who found us in the dark?"

Their dad said, "The entire village, all your friends and neighbors love you and turned out to find you because you were lost. We were led by these two young men Jesus and John—without them we would not have found you until daylight and maybe not then. We thought you went in the other direction so we probably would have spent days looking in the wrong direction. So, if you are ever in any doubt, follow these two men—Jesus and John."

(End)

+++++++++++++++++++++

## #38.	YOUNG JESUS AND JOHN—MIDWIFE (Fiction) July 2020

As young Jesus and John were whistling and walking along a seldom-traveled trail, they came upon a pregnant woman and pregnant donkey both lying down under a tree beside a small stream. The woman said, "Please don't ask if we need help. Of course we need help! We have each gone into labor and each of our little ones is turned wrong meaning you young men will need to help turn them around inside us so they can be born properly. And I see that look in your eyes--don't you dare run away!"

In unison, "Yes Mam". (They were raised proper Southern mannerly Jewish.)

Jesus said, "I'll help the donkey."

John adamantly said, "No. I will. I'm better with animals than with women."

Jesus replied, "Well, that's true for Me too and for every man."

John: No. You help the lady.

Woman: Stop bickering! You—what's Your name—Jesus—get over here, now!

Jesus: Yes Mam.

Woman: Jehovah sent You to help me through this.

Jesus: (Mumbling): I don't think Dad would do that to Me.

Woman: What?

Jesus: Oh Nothing. Tell me what to do.

There was much gymnastics, twisting, contortions, maneuvering, pain, pushing, and finally success. Jesus was touched by the holy moment of birth of a new baby and the love shining so deeply in the mother's eyes—the compassion ran deep and strong. He told her, He'd give her a few minutes alone with her new baby, to call when she needed help. She nodded with glistening eyes.

After a few deep breaths, Jesus stepped over to see if John needed any help. John had a special touch with animals. The donkey had calmed down and had let John help turn the foal and it had just been born too.

They stood smiling and marveling at Jehovah's miracle of new life.

Then Jesus said, "I guess we can say each of us is a midwife. But next time you get the woman."

John: (laughing) Ok. Next time.

(End)

++++++++++++++++++++++++

#39.   YOUNG JESUS AND JOHN—FIREFIGHTERS (Fiction)   July 2020

As young Jesus and John camped near the Jordan River, their instincts awakened them as they smelled smoke. They were instantly on full alert—fire coming toward them and the nearby village. One would warn any homeowners and campers in the path while the other would warn the village.

Once awakened the village was in a panic and totally disorganized.   Jesus and John had rejoined and shouted above the noise finally getting everyone's attention. They organized a bucket brigade to establish a defensive line to protect the village. They also told some men to set back fires so the fire would burn itself out. This idea met with some resistance but time was running out so Jesus and John took off and set the fires on their own—action over argument.

The embers were blowing in front of the approaching fire and the villagers were beating them out and pouring water on their homes and praying the back fires would work.

The smoke was stifling, choking but they had no choice— run and lose everything or fight and hope to save it. They were fortunate, they had the river as their last resort.

Finally, through the smoke they began to see a lessening of the fire—the back fires had worked. They rushed out to stamp the monster to death before it could come back to life—every ember quenched. Finally, the dawn came—

tired, weary, but triumphant, they gathered together and gave thanks to Yahweh, to each other for banding together and special thanks to Jesus and John for their early warning and their decisive, correct leadership and working shoulder to shoulder with them. They said "We will stand with you anytime Jesus and John—but let's clean ourselves up first."

(End)

++++++++++++++++++++++++++++

#40. YOUNG JESUS AND JOHN—DRIVE A CHARIOT (Fiction) July 2020

As young Jesus and John walked down a narrow road they had to jump aside to avoid an onrushing Roman chariot. They shouted, "Slow down! Sharp curve!" to no avail. They turned and ran back the way they had just come knowing they would find a crashed chariot, which they did. The driver was lying, injured on the ground and they rushed to his side. His arm was broken and, while he was unconscious, they set it, wrapped splints around it to keep it in place and put his arm in a sling. They patched up some cuts and scratches and gave him some water when he awakened with a start, asking who they were and what they wanted and ordering them to help him stand up. They did and he promptly slithered back down. After a few more drinks of water, he tried again.

He thanked them for setting his arm and helping him. He asked if they could right his chariot that he had urgent messages to deliver.   The chariot needed a bit of carpenter's ministrations but was ready to go after a bit but Jesus and John pointed out that he was not going to be able to drive.

An up and coming Roman officer unable to complete his mission, now looked desperately at Jesus and John and asked, "Would you two drive the chariot with me to my destination, please? I cannot fail? When you get older you may understand the importance of completing your mission."

Jesus and John, exchanged knowing looks, nodded and said, "Let's go".

They took turns driving the chariot and couldn't help laughing as the rode and drove—and since the officer was in a hurry, they bid the horse go faster and faster—it was their fastest ride ever—one they often remembered with fondness and smiles. Jesus said he was the better driver but John disagreed. The horse didn't like any of the three drivers, he was just totally exhausted when they arrived.

Note: Jesus and John spent time cooling the horse down and giving him a special meal of oats plus rubbing him down. The officer thanked them, rewarded them and had them dine and stay overnight with him and other soldiers, thus giving Jesus and John some insight into Roman soldiers.

(End).

+++++++++++++++++++++++++++++++++++

#41. YOUNG JESUS AND JOHN—OLD SHEPHERD (Fiction) July 2020

Young Jesus and John saw a large herd of sheep in the distance and decided to spend some time with the shepherds. They enjoyed working with the men and learning about the sheep, their habits and peculiarities. At night they enjoyed listening to the shepherds especially since a couple could sing some ancient shepherd tunes handed down from the time of David when he was a shepherd. They began to learn parts of some of the songs which they learned the sheep liked as the songs calmed and quieted them.

One night, an older shepherd pointed to a bright star and began telling of a bright star nearly 20 years ago. On that night an angel suddenly appeared telling him and the others not to be afraid that a Savior had been born in David's town, Bethlehem, to go and find Him lying in a manger. Then the sky was filled with angels singing the most magnificent and glorious songs ever heard, praising Jehovah and saying Peace on Earth. Good Will to Men.

Jesus and John had crept closer and were barely breathing

The old shepherd continued, "We were stunned! I couldn't breathe. Finally, I tried to speak and wobbled over to get a drink of water. Then I said, 'Let's Go see the Messiah, that has been born! This is the chance of a lifetime! We few have been blessed with this wonderful news. Come let's go! NOW!' That broke the trance or spell and we were off. Running as fast as we could. When we got to Bethlehem, we found the stable and there was the man—his name was Joseph, the mother—her name was Mary, and she was holding The Baby—the Messiah. After some time we told them about the angels and why we came. The Holy Mother let us take turns holding The Baby. (He cradled his arms as if holding a baby.) I, even I, got to hold Him, The Messiah—it was the holiest moment of my life—I kissed Him on the forehead. I remember it every day—I tell everyone, "The Messiah has come—ready your hearts. He is here—I held Him". But mostly they just think it's the foolish talk and ramblings of an old man. But it happened."

Jesus whispered, "I know. Thank you for holding Me."

The shepherd looked startled as John whispered, "He is the Messiah."

Jesus said, "Come aside so we can talk. You are the only shepherd eyewitness I have ever met since I've come of age. Tell us every detail you can remember."

Over the next few days, the shepherd continued to pour out memories of that night and all the details, many of which he had forgotten. He even made crude drawing of the scenes of the angels, the stable, Joseph, Mary and Jesus, and the others around the stable. He told of the other shepherds later drifting away, some getting married, others like himself, going to different places, some changing jobs. John, but especially Jesus, enjoyed their visit with the old shepherd and reluctantly went on their way but not before Jesus gave the shepherd a carving of an angel and the Baby in the manger which he treasured.

(End)

++++++++++++++++++++++

#42. YOUNG JESUS AND JOHN—WORK IN A VINEYARD (Fiction) August 2020

Excitement increased as harvesting time neared because Jesus and each of His siblings who were old enough, could earn a little extra money by working in the fields. Though it was hard, dirty, sweaty work, they enjoyed it because it was something different, they would meet their friends and relatives, they got free lunch or dinner on the ground, and they earned money, some of which they contributed to the household income but some of which they kept for their own. Spending money—a rare treat.

Cousin John met them at the vineyard and proved to be a sturdy and capable worker. Few could match his skill and speed and at the end of the day he always seemed to have produced the most. He was usually quite serious about his work so everyone was surprised when toward the end of the last day he started throwing grapes at everyone which led to a free-for-all grape throwing contest with everyone laughing and being purpled. The owner was a good sport and joined in and thanked everyone for the best harvest ever.

He then asked them to help with the next steps which they all enjoyed. The girls especially liked stomping grapes barefoot to squeeze the juice out, after being teased about washing their feet first.

Jesus and John were particularly interested in learning every facet of the vineyard business. They learned firsthand not to put new wine in old wineskins. They were surprised that some wine tasted so much better than other wines. They learned there was work to tending the vines year round, not just during the harvest and how to store wine and so much more. The owner was glad to have such willing workers learning the business.

++++++++++++

During other harvest times, the family members would work helping harvest wheat, corn, oats, potatoes, or whatever needed extra "hands". They each could do various age-appropriate jobs and get paid accordingly. Some just worked but Jesus and John were always eager to learn everything about the entire business. For example, preparing the field, sewing the wheat, keeping the weeds and birds out, praying for rain, harvesting, threshing, winnowing the wheat with the aid of a gentle breeze, and saving the best seeds for next year's crop. Grinding the wheat into meal, making the meal into bread and so much more.   It was hard work, year round—they admired the farmers and were glad to work with them and learn of their labors and lives.

These were people Jesus and John identified with—grew up with—labored with—were one with—these were people they loved dearly.   These years helped prepare them for their coming missions.

(End)

(Note: Growing up, children of farmers often worked in the fields harvesting cotton, peanuts, corn, etc.,   My wife said she and her siblings often made spending money (and got fed) by harvesting tobacco. So maybe Jesus and His siblings harvested crops.)

+++++++++++++++++++++++++

#43. <u>YOUNG JESUS AND JOHN—VISIT A PRISON</u>. (Fiction) August 2020

As they gathered for supper, Mary explained that her cousin Eve and her two children would have nowhere to live since her husband was going to prison.

James chimed in, "We could clean out that old barn where the donkey stayed before he died, and we could maybe fix it up and add a room and they could live there. They could share our outhouse, our well, garden food, and we have extra blankets."

Everyone joined in saying they would help, and so they set to work the next day and Eve and family moved in right away with Mary until their new home was ready. She thanked them over and over. She felt disgraced because her husband was in prison. All her women friends, except Mary and Elizabeth, had turned their backs on her and, except for Mary and Joseph, she and her two children would have struggled to survive.

Eve visited her husband in prison as often as she could but she always returned weeping and broken hearted with tales of how terrible conditions were in the prison. The inmates were fed a watery soup which caused them all to lose weight, they were worked harshly and beaten which produced open, untreated sores, and they slept on soiled hay. Often the guards took half of what little she brought to her husband and harassed her before letting her see him.

Now, young Jesus and John were lugging bundles of food, blankets, clothing, medicines, etc., as they followed Eve on a trip to the prison. The supplies Jesus and John were bringing were some they had acquired from their own homes first. Then they had gone to neighbors asking for donations. Interestingly, when someone came to the door, John started preaching loud and strong, and they were often moved to make donations—whether in the spirit of generosity or just to get him to move along.

This was their first visit and they were ill prepared for what they encountered. The stench alone was enough to cause them to wonder how 'could humans treat other humans this way'. The guards took one look at their stern faces and quickly assisted them in dispersing the supplies to those most in need. With Jesus and John telling the inmates of Jehovah's love, they readily shared the food and other supplies, something new and unusual inside the prison. Jesus and John proved very tender and adept at treating and binding up the wounds. The blankets were welcomed and shared so that some slept without shivering for the first time since being there. Together they sang songs, repeated Psalms, and said prayers, and for the first time hate and anger subsided within those walls.

Later, when alone, Jesus and John wept. The next day they got others to help them gather hay for the prisoners to sleep on. Then they gathered brooms, mops, cleaning supplies and went back to the prison and helped prisoners clean each cell and gave each fresh sleeping hay. With a bit of persuasion, the guards began to take an interest in keeping things that way.

When Jesus and John had told Mary and Elizabeth about the conditions, they started a campaign. After besieging the local authorities, the synagogue, and neighbors, they were finally able to effect small changes. Some of Eve's former friends now realized it was not her fault, that it could happen to them and they began to help out. The synagogue raised money for family members of those in prison and petitioned the prison authorities to improve conditions. After all this effort, the prison conditions were still bad, but not as terrible. Now more visitors came bearing food and supplies which improved their strength and health almost immediately.

As things improved, the prisoners knew it started with Jesus and John. They would long remember those two young men who came amongst them, fed them, cleaned them, did not despise them, treated them as human beings not something to be locked away in a dirty prison and forgotten. Those young men treated them with dignity and respect, something they had not felt in a long, long time. Jesus and John—why couldn't everyone be like them?

(End)

Note: The prison visits would have an impact on both John and Jesus and their ministries*.

(Author's Comment: On our home place, there were two old houses, one had once been a barn. My parents generously allowed various relatives to live there as needed—I'm sure rent free. One family was a widowed aunt another was a cousin with children whose husband was in prison. Remembering these, to honor my parents, I went back and added the "barn house" for Eve in this story.)

*Matt 25: 43 I was a stranger and you did not take Me in, I was naked and you did not clothe Me, I was sick and in prison and you did not visit Me.' 44 And they too will reply, 'Lord, when did we see You hungry or thirsty or a stranger or naked or sick or in prison, and did not minister to You?' 45Then the King will answer, 'Truly I tell you, whatever you did not do for one of the least of these, you did not do for Me.'…

+++

#44.   YOUNG JESUS MAKES SHOES FOR JOHN (Fiction) August 2020

As young Jesus and John walked down a seldom traveled road, they spoke to a Rabbi hurrying on his way and then a Levite, also in a hurry. Then they rounded a curve in the road and found a bleeding, unconscious, naked (except for his insignia) Roman soldier lying on the ground. Without hesitation, they stopped his bleeding, gave him the clothes off their backs, gave him water and they made a litter with which to carry him. They carried him for several hours until they reached a place that would accept him and care for him until he was well.

They did not have enough money to stay in the same place so they camped outside for a few days until their patient improved. Jesus always carried a few basic woodworking tools, just in case. He measured the man's feet and His and John's. Since John's feet were the right size, John gave up his shoes while Jesus made him a new pair—the patient getting the more comfortable pair.

Jesus said "I'm not a shoe maker but maybe these will do until you can get a real pair." Jesus cut, whittled and trimmed and had the soles made out of wood in short order. Then he found some cord to lace them up and John was no longer barefoot.

John tried them out and smiled saying, "They do make a distinct clop clop sound and are stiff as a board but other than that, they work great. Who else can say they have a pair of shoes made by Jesus? Thank you."

Jesus and John had many conversations with their patient about Jehovah and how He loved everyone and that He was a God of Love, forgiveness, mercy, peace. At night he thought about what they said and wondered, in all the land, these two men were probably the only ones that would have helped him, a despised Roman soldier. Did this God of theirs send them to help him? If so, why? These two sure did make him think?

A few days later, their patient improved and went on his way with many thanks. He said he would long remember the names of John and Jesus.

(End)

++++++++++++++++++++++++++

Note: John the Baptist still wore those shoes—his favorite pair--the day Jesus came to the Jordan to be baptized. (Matt 3:14)

Note: (Fiction)   At the cross, that same solder was the Centurion who, with a broken heart, said with conviction "Truly, this was the Son of God!" (Matt 27:54) ((Epilog: Fiction: And for the rest of his life he told the story of how a young Jesus and John the Baptist patched him up and how he watched Jesus die on the cross and then saw Jesus alive again after He arose from the dead. This same Jesus—ALIVE!   He became known as "The Christian Centurion" and won many to Christ. His question of "why" was answered.))

++
+

++
+++++++++++++++++++

#45. YOUNG JESUS AND JOHN— A DYING MAN (Fiction) Aug 2020

"My husband is dying! He wants to confess his sins to anyone. You look like holy men. Please come help. Hurry! My children are next door. He has said goodbye to them and to me but now he wants to unburden his past."

Young Jesus and John rushed to her house near the Jordan River and knew instantly the smell of rotting flesh, gangrene and after a quick glance knew her husband's time was very short.

He said through labored breaths, "Thank you for coming. Before I meet Jehovah, I want to confess and repent of my sins." And he did to Jesus and John. Then he thanked them again and stared at John and said, "My mother knew Elizabeth and Zechariah and told me I'd meet their son John one day and I'd recognize him and he would be a great prophet in Israel. I thought she was being foolish but now I know she was right. Your name is John isn't it?"

John: Yes, I am John and this is Jesus, the long-awaited Messiah. We have not started our missions. Yes I will be a prophet.

Dying Man: (Laughing) My mother was right. I am blessed to meet you John and You Jesus. My soul has been cleansed of my sins. I could die in peace if I knew my family would be taken care of.

Jesus: Do not worry about your family.

Man: You have not started your missions yet. But would you take me down to the Jordan and baptize me. I know my soul has been cleansed of my sins but I'd feel better and I think my wife and children would too if they saw me baptized as a sign that Yahweh has washed away my sins. John, maybe I can be the first that you baptize.

So, Jesus and John carried him on his bed down to the Jordan River—over the objections of his wife. A crowd gathered including his physician who strongly objected but the man told him and his wife in a loud voice to be quiet that this is what he wanted to do. Jesus and John helped him into the river, repeated some scriptures, said some prayers and John baptized him. Then they helped him back into his bed and carried him back to his house and dried him off. The man thanked them again and dropped off to sleep. Jesus and John said goodbye to his wife and children and went on their way.

A short ways down the road, Jesus said, "You did well with your first baptism. Jehovah is well pleased."

John: I felt Your healing. He will be amazed in the morning. In the future, I hope the people don't expect all my baptisms to be healings of the body.

Jesus: And to think, John, he's been expecting to meet you all his life because of his mother's faith. Mother's have a tremendous influence.

(End)

+++++++++++++++++++++++++++++++

#46.   YOUNG JESUS AND JOHN—BEES AND A DRUNK (Fiction) Aug 2020

As young Jesus and John walked down and empty trail, suddenly they saw and heard a large swarm of bees coming toward them.

Jesus said: John, you are the bee expert, what do you plan to do?

John: This bee expert is GETTING OUT OF THE WAY. And he dove into the ditch with Jesus right behind him

In the ditch, Jesus said: I'm glad I was with a bee expert, otherwise I might not have known what to do.

John: (Laughing) Oh You are a smart person, I think You would have figured it out. (As they both laughed and rolled and wrestled in the ditch.)

After a bit they got back on the trail with John following the hum of the hive as a future source of honey. They hadn't gone far before they encountered an upturned cart with a man and woman lying on the side of the trail. Their donkey had not been able to avoid the swarm. Jesus and John quickly helped the man and woman who were only slightly injured. Then they proceeded to untangle the bucking, braying donkey. With calmness and soothing words they carefully untangled the lines and traces and finally got the badly stung animal back in harness. They used their water to make some mud to apply to its stings which eased the pain.

The couple was shaken up and appreciated Jesus and John escorting them to a house on the trail where they all stayed the night. The hosts were gracious, provided a meal for everyone, and floor pallets for their guests. Just as everyone started to settled down, the grown son of their host burst in drunk, quarreling and shouting. Jesus and John stepped defensively between him and his parents to which he sneered, drew back a fist but then something in their eyes got through his befuddled brain. He blinked, stepped back and asked, "Who are You?" He promptly passed out.

His parents apologized, put a blanket over him and thanked Jesus and John. Perceiving them to be more than mere travelers they asked if they could help their son end his drinking, and rid himself of his demons.

Jesus and John held their hands, prayed, then said, "Your son has invited this demon into his body and allowed it to control him. This addiction, this disease is a self-induced one. You are more concerned about his health than he is. He must first admit he has a problem. Your love and faith are wonderful. When he is ready to seek help, then he can begin to get better. If you like, we will take him with us into the wilderness where he will have only water to drink. The wilderness can be a stern teacher but can also dry out the body and cleanse the soul. He may hate you for it but in time your real son may return to you."

They both responded, "Yes, take him, now, this instant. Please."

The three left the next morning with the son griping, complaining and threatening but not willing to test either Jesus or John. They encountered a sandstorm and the son thought they were lost (he was) and were going to die but finally they were in a small cave with water and shortly a small fire and a bit to eat. Next morning, he was unprepared for the deafening quiet and emptiness. He asked to go home but was put to work digging a trench for the well water. Over the next many days he helped bring rocks to line the well and the trench so water could be left standing for wild animals to drink. At night, he was amazed at the brightness of the desert stars and began to ask the names of some. He soon learned how to navigate by the stars and found himself eager to learn more about the wilderness. When asked what he would do with his life, he said he would like to work with animals. The local stable was always looking for help---the work couldn't be any harder than what he had been doing. Or maybe he'd try working with a caravan—he liked the wilderness—one thing for sure, he would never drink again because his parents would call them to come drag him out here again. And they all laughed.

When they returned, his parents were astonished. They repeated over and over, "Thank you Jesus and John. You have saved our son's life. Thank you."

(End)

(Comment: Was on the edge of a ball field in high school when a swarm of bees came by. Someone yelled, "lay down on the ground".   Added the drug addiction because every family is affected by this terrible demon. I hope Jesus will forgive me for presuming to put words in His mouth.)

++

#47.   MARY   ENCOUNTERS   UNMARRIED EXPECTING GIRL (Fiction)   Aug 2020

As Mary was returning from a rare visit to a quiet place of solitude, she heard someone sobbing. She approached quietly and found a very young, pregnant girl. After a few moments, Mary cleared her throat and asked if she could help.

Girl: Nobody can help. I'm expecting a baby and I'm not married.   The father laughed and said it probably was someone else's. I thought he was nice. I have no parents, no aunts or relatives, nobody.   I cannot go to the synagogue. I have done a terrible thing and Jehovah has deserted me—which I deserve.

Mary: Where do you live?

Girl: Nowhere. I have been just roaming. I had a place and a job but they kicked me out when they discovered my condition. Now I'm just living in the woods. I sneak into town to get food from the garbage heap or beg or whatever. When people see I'm pregnant they—they... (Sniff) A nice lady like you --you just don't know how humiliating it is—people making jokes, talking behind your back, laughing at you.

Mary: Believe me I know. Come, little one, come with me. You can stay with us. We have an old barn that we fixed up for a mother of two whose husband is in prison. They'll welcome you and just love you to a frazzle. She will love to have a young woman to talk to and she and I will coach you through childbirth and raising a baby. We will help you learn how to cook, sew, and learn a trade to earn enough money to support yourself, all in due time.

Girl: You'd do that for me? A stranger?

Mary: Yes. Yahweh has not abandoned you. He sent me to you. He loves everyone, especially unmarried girls who are expecting. My husband and sons are carpenters. We will add another room onto the barn for you and your baby---who by the way, won't be the first baby born in a barn.

(End)

#48. YOUNG JESUS AND JOHN—WIDOW IN COURT—PAINTED STONES (Fiction) Aug 2020

"Get out! It is no longer your house, it is mine!" said the rude banker who calmed down when young Jesus and John stepped to the woman's defense. He was accustomed to men of all ages cowering before him because his money gave him power and control but these two stern youngsters were not frightened but in fact frightened him.

He blustered, "I loaned her money when her husband died, she has not paid it back, so her house is now mine. It's all legal. See, here is the paperwork.   Come, we will go to court to make it final."

After glancing at the papers, Jesus said, "This says she has three days after the judge's final decision which is today. So she has at least three more days, yet you wanted her out today."

"Well, what's three more days?   She doesn't have the money."

Jesus said, "A lot can happen in three days—the whole world can change in three days."

John: Mam, if you like, we will go with you to court.

Lady: Oh thank you. My neighbor will keep my little girl.

In court—Judge: Mam, since you cannot pay, I must rule that the property is his. You must vacate in three days. I'm sorry.

Lady: But Judge, where will I go? I have no relatives? No friends can afford to take me in—what am I going to do?

Judge: Go to the synagogue—perhaps they can help.

Outside—Jesus: Mam, John and I will help you move to My house. We are a family of carpenters, we have added rooms on to an old barn and we will add another for you. Glad you have some chickens, they'll fit right in with ours.

And that is what happened, except Joseph and family added two more rooms anticipating Jehovah would send another homeless family their way sooner or later, so why not be ready. They even built a long connected porch across the front of all the rooms, giving the children a nice shaded place to play and the mothers a convenient place to visit, shell peas and butterbeans, shuck corn, and do many other chores.

All the orphans and children of prisoners learned to work hard at age-appropriate tasks. Two of the boys were old enough to go exploring on their own and found a large deposit of smooth river rocks. (They discussed later and found out maybe ages ago a river ran through that area and left the rocks.) The boys used a small wagon to bring several loads to their house hoping to have a rock floor for their mom, but when they tried placing them, the rocks tilted and wobbled too much when stepped on. But they liked the rocks.

They asked Joseph if they could use some of his paint. He gave them the right kind and they started painting Psalms on the stones. They gave a painted stone to Mary, their moms and each of the other widows to place outside their doors. They were painting when James happened by and said maybe the stone mason in town would buy some of the unpainted stones. So the three took a wagon load to the village stone mason, who did indeed like them. He and his wife both liked the painted stones also. The mason said he could use those river stones in special places such as the top of walls or at entrances. They negotiated a price on some stones thinking several wagon loads when the younger suggested a better deal for them. They would use the mason's donkey and cart to haul the stones, bringing more, quicker and easier for them. The mason laughed and agreed and insisted they all first come eat lunch.

During lunch, his wife talked more and more about painting the stones and having some for sale at the shops near the streets where travelers would see them, maybe paint some in different languages—puzzled looks. She said maybe she would open a shop at the edge of town selling the rocks and other things. The mason said there might not be enough stones.

After a few days, the mason realized how much he and his wife liked the two boys. They gave all the money they made to their moms. He talked to their moms and asked if they could work as apprentices in the stone mason business—if they wanted to. It was a skilled trade they could learn and in time would allow them to support themselves and their moms. Each mom broke down in tears and thanked him for treating her orphan boy or son of a prisoner as a regular boy and giving them this wonderful opportunity.

Each boy learned the stone mason business but everyone was surprised that the painted stone business continued to flourish—so much so that they got their sisters and others in the "Barn House" to help paint rocks.

Jesus and John and the other widows tried to alert every new widow to the dangers of signing loans with bankers and they also steered them to the ever growing "Barn House."

(End)

+++++++++++++++++++

#49.   YOUNG JESUS AND JOHN FIND A BABY (Fiction) Aug 2020

John said, "Listen. Did you hear that? It sounded like a baby. Come on." And he was off at a fast pace with Jesus close behind, while marveling at John's keen wilderness hearing. A few minutes later they stopped and this time they both heard the unmistakable sounds of a baby which led them to the abandoned newborn.

They carefully checked the child who seemed healthy but hungry, wrapped warmly in clothing of a Samaritan. The child was clearly of mixed parentage which explained why the desperate mother did not take the child to the synagogue which should welcome everyone but sadly did not.

John said the mother had left enough tracks that he could follow her for some distance and Jesus said He would take the baby to His mother which was in the direction of the tracks so they traveled together and stopped to let the baby rest.

John said, "I had a very loving mother—maybe even doting or smothering mother so I knew I was loved. And Dad knew the scriptures would be important in my life work so he drilled and drilled me until I knew them by heart. He sought solitude in the wilderness where he communed with Jehovah and at an early age took me with him, teaching me the stars and helping me develop a love of the desert. He never said it, but I knew my dad loved me. I grew up in a home filled with love and affection. Had I been abandoned as this baby, I would have been very different with less love and compassion for my fellow man—probably with much anger and bitterness. Love in a home is so important. Your family is helping those families so much and maybe this one too. I hope to be able to track the mother and let her know her child is safe. That would ease a lifetime burden."

Jesus: When you find where she is, come to Mom's and we will go talk to her together.

At Mary's, Jesus handed her the baby and told her about finding the child.

Mary: Oh the poor thing and the mother must be desperate, alone, forsaken and now she will be haunted by what she has done. I hope You and John can find her and bring her here to live. The other room is ready for her and her child.

Just then John arrived saying he knew where she worked, and they left with Mary's blessings.

When they met the new mother, she had tear streaks on her face and she quickly gasped when they showed her the little blanket in which she had wrapped her baby. They assured her the baby was safe and she poured out her heart saying she could not afford to keep the baby. She said she had no family, no friends, nobody in the world cared if she and her baby lived or died and she knew the synagogue was closed to them so she did the unthinkable, the unforgiveable and now not only did the Jews despise her and all Samaritans but their Jehovah would despise her and never look at her.

Jesus said, "We are looking at you. Jehovah looks at you and loves you. He forgives you. He wants you to be a good mother. You have a second chance. My family has a room that we added on to a barn knowing Jehovah would send us someone to live in it. He sent you and your child to us. So gather your things right now and come with us. It will be tough and you will have to work hard.

New Mom: Are you sure? I'm a Samaritan as is my child and you are a Jew.

Jesus: In the other rooms of the barn house, there are two widow families, and one woman whose husband is in prison. We are carpenters and we will make you a rocking chair in which you can rock your baby to your heart's content.

New Mom: But they are all proper Jews and won't want to associate with us.

Jesus: (Smiling) John, I think we forgot to check to see if they are proper Jews. All we know is they needed a home, as you do. So, come, John and I will carry your things. My Mother has your baby and she is waiting to welcome you to your new home and your new life.

(End)

Note: Everyone enjoyed having a new baby to rock—and rock they did. The young girls especially liked having a live " baby doll" to dress up and play with.

(The carpenters built a couple more rooms onto the Barn House.)

Epilog: She had an unknown superior talent for pottery which she eventually displayed in a shop along a road out-of-towners traveled.   One man from out of town kept coming back and finally asked if she were married. She then gave her total history including her baby, expecting that to end his visit. His comment, "Good, so you are not married and I can come calling, how about tonight." She explained again and he told of his past and they agreed to meet and kept meeting, Though they did not "live happily ever after," they did work hard at their marriage and got through the rough patches together. They named their first son "John" 'because he tracked me down when I needed it.'

+++++++++++++++++++++++++

#50. YOUNG JESUS AND JOHN—AN OLD MAN (Fiction) Aug 2020

An old man struggled along until he sort of sat/collapsed down on a rock ahead of young Jesus and John. When they offered him some of their water he gladly accepted as well as some of their food. Then without prompting, he told them he had been a good farmer for many years but his children did not want to farm and had moved far away to the cities and he had lost contact with them. His wife had died and he had been alone for some years. As he aged he was only able to farm enough to feed himself but not enough to pay the taxes. So now they had kicked him out of his home—for taxes. His life time of work in these few bundles at his feet and "nowhere to lay my head".

He said, "Nobody wants old people! We are just in the way. Enjoy your youth. If you get to grow old, one day you will remember what I said: Nobody wants old people!"

Jesus: Well we want you. We have a room for you and we need someone who knows what he is doing to help in our garden. We will put you to work tomorrow morning as soon as the rooster crows. John and I will help you carry your things."

John: Do you know how to grow peanuts? I'd sure like some boiled peanuts. And sweet potatoes. My mom used to make sweet potato biscuits that were so good.

Old man: Oh yes. They are one of my favorites. And sweet potatoes too. Lets go. Time to plant both. And tomatoes too.

And they were off—the old man had a skip in his step and a light in his eye. He fit right in with the growing Barn House families. He hinted that he'd like a rocking chair too and the carpenters had one for him in no time. He proved to be a good farmer who was adept at passing on that knowledge to eager ears who put it to good use in an ever expanding garden—seemed he helped everyone have a "green" thumb.

Epilog: The old man was the first to enter a "Retirement Home". From time to time the widows would meet someone, marry and move away leaving a vacant room which was never vacant long.

++++++++++++++++

#51.   YOUNG JESUS AND JOHN—PUPPIES (Fiction) Aug 2020

They could not believe it—a whole litter of puppies had been abandoned in the middle of nowhere—just left out there by themselves to starve. The puppies leaped onto Jesus and John as they knelt to pet and speak to them and give them some water which they thirstily lapped up in a hurry.

They looked at each other and John said, "Well we can't just leave them here."

Jesus said, "I know. I was thinking, those kids back at our Barn House have never owned anything, especially a pet. I remember how much you loved your dog."

John smiled, remembering and said, "Just what your Mother will want, more mouths to feed. And you know they will all want the same puppy. How are You going to decide which child gets which puppy?"

Jesus laughed and said, "That's easy. I'll tell them that the young prophet John has determined which puppy wants each of them."

John replied, "As usual, You are way ahead of me. How are we going to carry all these pups? Maybe use our cloaks to make a litter for the litter of pups."

When they got to Jesus' home, they called everyone together and said they had a surprise for the children. When they undid their cloaks and the puppies tumbled out, there were wild squeals of laughter, excitement, happiness and downright joy to the bottom of their hearts. Turns out the pups managed to pick out their new owners and John did not have to use his prophetic wisdom to help out. Any leftover pups were fostered till new permanent residents arrived.

Jesus and John knew what the children's reaction would be but were surprised at similar and deeper emotional outbursts by their mothers. They realized a mother's (a parent's) greatest joy comes when her child is happy, and in this case the child had received a wonderful present that the mother could never have afforded and their child's overwhelming happiness made mom's heart just overflow uncontrollably. A mother's love—close to the heart of God.

(End)

Note: My friend Kathy and I walk around a pond where some goslings were raised and the idea first came that they'd find goslings, but puppies worked better. The last paragraph came as I tried to put into words a parent's (my) joy at their child's happiness, especially at receiving a gift we could never afford. Just thought—<u>Jesus is the gift</u> we could never afford.

++ +++++++++++++++++

#52.   YOUNG JESUS AND JOHN—LATE TO THE HARVEST   (Fiction)   Sep 2020

"Come help with the harvest. I implore you. I need every available hand to come before the rains start. Even though the day is half over, I'll pay you a full day's pay. Come! Now!" said the desperate land owner.

So young Jesus and John went late to the harvest.

As they rushed along he noticed their rough, strong hands and thought they'd harvest more in a couple of hours than the village lay-abouts would in a day. And he was right.

Jesus and John quickly went to work noticing a group in another part of the field who appeared tired and, judging by their clothing, were from town. The village group were slowly working individually and not getting much done. Jesus and John worked as a team and in no time had harvested a large amount, which was noticed by the villagers, especially the youngest of the group, who commented, "They are working as a team and producing so much more that way. Come on let's do the same." And their production increased immediately, much to their delight. The youngest said "This is the first time in a long time I've gotten a full day job and I want the boss to know I worked hard and did a good job. Working as a team like this will help him know each of us did our best and that we are good workers and maybe he will hire us again. I need the money and as many jobs as I can get. So come on, let's harvest this field." And they did.

The owner was delighted and thanked them for their hard work. He paid them all a bonus and had them stay for supper and had quarters for any that wanted to stay overnight. Jesus and John ate with the villagers and learned their stories, especially the younger man whose father was in prison so he was desperately trying to support his mother and rest of the family, with up and down success. The other villagers complimented him on getting them to work as a team and working harder to finish the harvest before the coming rains.

Later the owner visited saying he needed someone full time if anyone was interested, looking directly at Jesus and John. They in turn suggested the young man who jumped (literally) at the chance and was hired on the spot. The four of them started talking and before he knew what had happened the owner had agreed to several things. He had been thinking about building new barns for his surplus harvest but somehow agreed to give the surplus to the poor including those in prison. He also agreed that the empty building/barn where the workers were sleeping that night would be converted into living quarters for his newest hire and his mother and family and his mother would be hired to cook and clean for the owner.

Next morning, the owner made sure all the workers had a generous breakfast before they left, thanked everyone, and loaned his new employee a horse and cart to bring his Mother and family to their new home right away. He said he never knew giving to the poor and helping others could feel so good. He looked at Jesus and John and wished them well and said "You are God-sent Harvesters. May Jehovah bless You in all You do. You are welcome here anytime."

(Note: Jesus and John secretly gave their wages to the poor and needy—widows, orphans, those in prison, the sick.)

The end.

+++++++++++++++++++++++++++++

#53. YOUNG JESUS AND JOHN AT A WEDDING (Fiction) Sep 2020

"Come join us on this happy day—this sad day—my daughter has gotten married and we are celebrating. We want everyone to celebrate with us. Come, come."

And so young Jesus and John unexpectedly joined a wedding celebration and had a happy time. After some hours, various people made toasts and speeches and John stood up and said, "I salute the couple and wish them the very best. Some might say these are terrible times to get married with Roman soldiers everywhere but I tell you that a new time is close at hand. A new day is coming where Jehovah will show His Love to this generation. The time to repent is at hand. Prepare your hearts for the Son of David is coming soon. This generation is a blessed generation. I offer my best wishes and blessings on this couple. May Jehovah favor them richly."

Some others spoke and then Jesus said, "Blessed are those who choose to hope, who choose joy , optimism, happiness as this couple has done by getting married. They have chosen each other and have looked to the future with hope—marriage personifies hope—marriage makes hope real—it bonds two people together in mind, body, soul, future, attitude, ---if one hurts the other hurts—if one is happy they are both happy. If you have never been in love you cannot understand what others mean when they say they are in love. Ahh but once you are in love—as these two are, then you know—you know. You might not be able to put it into words but you know what love is. And you have a tiny glimpse of Jehovah's love for each of you—all of you. Always remember God Loves you. And remember what John said.

Again I say, Blessed are those who choose hope.

(End)

NOTE: Those at the wedding who really listened to what John and Jesus said were surprised and even stunned. Jesus and John left before more questions could be asked but some were excited that Jehovah would be blessing them with love within this generation. So they told others and began preparing their hearts.

Author's comment: I am not worthy and am reluctant to put my words in Jesus' mouth. Because of that, I thought about deleting this story. I hope Jesus will forgive me if it is unworthy.

+++

#54.   YOUNG JESUS AND JOHN—JAMES JOINS THEM IN THE WILDERNESS (Fiction) Sep 2020

James was trying not to show his excitement at getting to join his older cousin John and big brother Jesus on this trip to the wilderness, where they had been a number of times. James wondered about their love of the desert region and now he would find out for himself. After a very long, hot, dry walk he was beginning to have his doubts—why not the Sea of Galilee, or the Jordan River or the cool mountains— well he certainly would not complain.   Finally they arrived—and James was disappointed—but after all, he told himself, this is a desert.

They quickly settled in, and James was thankful there was at least a well which he didn't drink dry but gave it a good try. Then he looked around and realized someone had dug the well and said, "You two dug this well didn't You. That was a lot of work. And you must be the ones that dug those other "angel" wells that just happened. Oh, Jesus, this is the little wind mill you made to draw the water up from the well to create this water flow for the animals and look some grass is growing over there near that rock pool—what a nice peaceful spot."

John: That spot is special; it is where we often go to pray. Prayer, solitude, communion with Jehovah—that is why I long for the wilderness—it restores my soul. Tonight you may join us if you like.

That night, the three went to the special spot—that holy ground—and knelt in prayer and discussion—hour after hour of prayer. James prayed but his prayers ended and he listened.   He heard them say "the people will expect a worldly kingdom---they will expect a Messiah that will overthrow the Romans---they will expect a worldly king. We must teach and show them Jehovah's kingdom is about Love and not of this world" At least James thought that is what he heard as he drifted off to sleep. During the night he awakened a few times, checked to see them still in prayer, and drifted back to sleep.

James awakened with the dawn and looked around to see John and Jesus arising from a night of prayer. All three went to the little rock pool and washed and refreshed themselves. They had breakfast—Mary always packed a heavy basket of goodies so her boys wouldn't go hungry—her biscuits were so good and John provided the wild honey.

Finally, James said, that when they prayed he realized their prayers were so ardent, from the depths of their souls that they seemed to merge with Jehovah's Spirit. During the night, he awakened and he thought their faces glowed during their prayers—but perhaps it was the moon shining on them. He went on saying, later he awakened and he thought he saw them talking to angels but maybe he dreamed that. And he added, "While here, I hope to learn how to pray more like You."

While there in the wilderness the three roamed around exploring and just soaking in the wonder of the desert. Often they would stop and look at a small bug, bush, or animal and talk about how Jehovah was so amazing to create such a variety of living things—and how truly amazing Life was—life in all its forms. Wow.

Before he knew it, James found himself liking the wilderness and wanting to stay longer. One night he could not sleep. He was thinking about John and Jesus. He had heard about their births and knew each was special, especially Jesus. He grew up with them and was very close to Jesus who would say or do something that by itself did not mean anything. But hearing them pray each night so strongly and sincerely and hearing them talk about what was to come—they had changed.   They were still his earthly cousin John and brother Jesus---but, but now James was beginning to have a growing conviction that each was to become so much more.   John clearly was a young prophet. Jesus was ….he dare not say what His birth and the scriptures said---

He finally went to sleep wondering, "What manner of Brother are You, my Brother Jesus?"

(Note: After Jesus' resurrection and ascension, James became convinced that Jesus his Brother was indeed the Son of God, the Messiah. James became a leader in the church in Jerusalem. When he could, he would go into the wilderness to the special place to renew his spirit and check on the windmill that still worked and clean out the rock pool and enjoy the glory of Jehovah's creations. And say, "I know now what manner of Brother You are My Lord and Savior Jesus Christ, the Living Son of the Living God.")

(End)

++++++++++++++++

#55.   YOUNG   JESUS   AND   JOHN—TWO ORPHANS—PIGGYBACK. (Fiction) Sep 2020

"Put that back. You know, 'Thou shall not steal.' Besides, we have some food and we will help you."

The young boy snarled, "All of them have said they wanted to help us after they beat me but they never helped us. Yes I know the commandment, "Thou shall not steal" but is there one that says "Thou shall not let your sister starve?" Go ahead beat me but I'll fight you!" as he put up his fists.

His sister said, "Brother these two are different, can't you see that? Don't be angry."

Brother: (Now in a rage at being an orphan, not being able to care for himself and his sister, no one helping them and everything boiling to a point.) Just leave us alone—go away—I'll knock you down—don't touch me.....

John lifted brother up to his eye level and calmly said, "We love you and your sister and we ARE going to help you. My Friend is sent from Jehovah to bring Love and Hope to all mankind. Now if you will stop struggling, we will give you some of our food and Jesus will take you to His Mother's house where you will have a home."

Brother was surprised at how strong John was and his strong, penetrating, calming words and suddenly he was no longer afraid—a great responsibility was being lifted from his young shoulders. They might have a home. He looked over at Jesus for assurance.

Jesus said: Mother will welcome you. Here is some food and water. Come let's go.

Jesus and John hoisted them onto their backs and carried them piggyback—first they took off running which brought squeals of laughter, cries of delight, tighter grips and even a few shouts of "faster faster" from their passengers who had not laughed in a long time. They felt safe and secure for the first time ever. After slowing to a walk, while the siblings ate and drank, Jesus prepared them for what to expect.

Jesus: When we get to Mom's, she will hug you and then have you bathe

Brother: I don't need a bath—boys don't need to bathe.

Jesus: She's my Mom and I will tell you something—do NOT try to get out of bathing. She is loving but stern. I and all my brothers and sisters always bathe and John too. (John nodded.) We are a family of carpenters and when a family needed a place to stay we changed an old barn into a place for them to live. Then added more rooms as others needed a place to stay.

Sister: Will they want orphans—we don't even know who our parents are. We have been called bad names.

Jesus: Some of the children that are there have no dad, one dad is in prison, some children are Samaritans, some Gentiles, some may have Roman fathers.

Brother: I thought Jews were supposed to hate Samaritans, Gentiles, and Romans. I'm not sure what we are.

Jesus: Jehovah created all of us and loves each of us—so we should too.

Brother: Love everybody? Even those who beat me and called us bad names? John, do you think that is possible?

John: Yes. With Him, He does it all the time—you will see.

Jesus: Remember do as Mom says, because in all these years I won a discussion with her just three times—wait, make that two, no just one, well actually never. So just do what she says. Right John.

John: Yes! Once we were so dirty, had been riding the goats, Jesus smelled, and maybe I did too, we were so tired we almost went to sleep at the supper table. We thought maybe Aunt Mary would let us go to bed without bathing but she sniffed and sent us off to bathe.

Jesus: You almost went to sleep bathing. But we bathed. Anyway, just do what Mom says.

John: You can call her Mrs. Mary, Aunt Mary, or Mother Mary—whatever the other children call her and what you like best but always be respectful. You and everyone will have chores to do—work in the garden, milk the goats or cow, feed the chickens, clean up around the house, and so on—do your job and more. Jesus is an excellent carpenter and one lady is a good potter others have other talents. You will find you are good at something and that may be how you will earn your living. Everyone works.

Jesus: Here we are. Mom, here are two wonderful youngsters we'd like you to meet.

Mary: Welcome. Come give me a hug.

And they did—a long, long hug. The first motherly hug they had had—as least that they could remember. They clung to her and she sensed they needed some mothering, so she sat and held them for a long time as Jesus shooed everyone else away to give them a bit of bonding time.

After a bit, while Jesus had dispatched someone to get some clothes for them, sure enough brother and sister came out heading to get a bath. Jesus paired them with someone about the same age to show them around and in short order they bathed and were just beginning to fit in.

Mary spoke to Jesus and John: Thank you for bring those two. They are tough to have survived all alone—totally alone. They needed me to hug and hold them—I could feel the fear and tension easing and dissolving. Now, finally, maybe they can be children for a while.

Jesus: Thanks Mom.

NOTE: In the kitchen Mary privately showed them how to wait till the meal was blessed, how to sit, how to properly hold eating utensils, and various other table manners so they would not be embarrassed at family meals. The first few nights, brother and sister slept together on floor pallets near the door with Mother Mary joining them until they felt genuinely secure enough to sleep in the respective boys and girls rooms. Mary realized they had never learned to read or write or play with other children. She enlisted the help of various children and adults to remedy all these situations, happily finding them to be quick learners and very smart-- perhaps their survival skills had activated their intellect too. Jesus carved them some animal figures—their first ever presents which they treasured. In short order, they settled in and were happy for the first time in their lives.

(End)

++

#56.   YOUNG JESUS AND JOHN—A PATCH OF FLOWERS AND A PINNACLE (Fiction) Sep 2020

Young John knelt to study the patch of spring flowers, then lay down to soak in their existence, as Jesus lay down beside him. After a time of meditation, John in reverent voice said, "Only Jehovah could create living flowers—so far beyond human comprehension. And look at that butterfly and honey bee—living testaments of Yahweh's unfathomable depths of love, life, and creation. Human minds are unable to understand even a tiny bit of I AM. Our languages are inadequate to allow us to praise Him as we would like to and as we should. We do not deserve the honor to say His Name—to speak to Him—He blesses us in so many ways such as allowing us to look upon His creations, such as this patch of flowers and be in awe."

Jesus: Solomon in all his glory was not arrayed like one of these. *

John: How can anyone look at Jehovah's creations and not believe in God. The Psalmist is correct, "The fool says in his heart, 'There is no God.'" **

Later from a pinnacle, they soaked in the panoramic view and absorbed the stillness and inner peace. They spent hours in meditation and prayer.

John said: This view is one of my favorites. I am in awe of Jehovah and His creations. At night I see the moon and stars and know they are countless distances away and I am humbled at Yahweh's vastness—and wonder why He loves us tiny humans so much. We don't deserve to even speak to Him but He welcomes us. Yet, through the genius of man, He has given us dominion over so much and so much more to come—may we use that genius with love.

Jesus: Yes, Love, that is our mission. Soon to start.

John: I like this wilderness so much. I think I understand why Moses was reluctant to leave. I could easily stay here the rest of my life. I also understand why Moses had doubts. What if I am not up to the job? I am basically a country boy, I'd rather stay here.

Jesus: I know. But your mission is out there, to prepare the people. John, Jehovah knew you before you were born and made you. You are a man sent from God. You have communed with Yahweh here in the wilderness and have heard His calling. You are His chosen prophet. You are ready. You will not fail. Your time draws nigh.

John: Thank You for Your reassurance. Let's enjoy this high point as long as we can. (After a time of silence.) Look, a falling star.

(End)

*Matthew 6:29

** Psalm 14:1

++

#57. YOUNG JESUS SAVES A BOY'S PET SHEEP (Fiction) Sep 2020

"I'm sorry son, your pet sheep is all we have to pay our taxes."

With tears in his eyes, the son looked at the tax collector and pleaded, "Mister, do you have to take my sheep. She is all I have in the world. I raised her from a lamb. Please."

"Rome demands taxes. Quit your crying. Grow up. Turn loose. Your sheep is now ours for taxes."

Young Jesus stepped between them, offered the tax collector a beautifully carved figure and said, "Will this do to pay their taxes in place of the sheep?"

The collector gasped as he grabbed the figure--realizing instantly that this was no mere carving but the work of a master craftsman worth several times the value of the sheep. As he examined the fine workmanship he quickly realized there might be more money to be made, so he said, "That is a fine sheep, in her prime. The wool will fetch a high price and the price of lamb chops are prime right now. "

The boy gasped, "Lamb chops! No!"

Jesus reached inside His cloak and retrieved two more figures saying, "This is all I have to give. Haven't you ever done something just to help someone and make them feel better—to help a fellow human being?"

The tax collector gave Jesus a puzzled look and said, "No. I'm a tax collector. All right these three carvings will take the place of this sheep though I'm losing money in the process. Don't expect such generosity in the future." And he went away—perhaps he would meet Jesus again someday.

The boy realized that his pet sheep had been saved at a sacrifice made by Jesus—he did not know how much but sensed quite a number of hours and skill had gone into those wooden carvings. He rushed into Jesus' arms saying over and over, "Thank You kind Sir, Thank You. My sheep was gone—gone for taxes and you saved her. I can never thank you enough. She was gone and now she is home. Come home with us and rejoice with us. Come meet my mother; she will want to thank you and fix you a big supper. Thank you again."

Note: The next day, as Jesus journeyed away, He saw a sign "Cook and workers wanted". He talked to the owner, told about the family he'd just left, about her good cooking, got an enthusiastic jobs commitment plus room and board and He retraced His steps to tell them the good news. They packed their few belongings, told their landlord, and with Jesus help, happily headed to their new future. Even the pet sheep seemed excited.

(End)

+++++++++++++++++++++++++++++

#58.

(skipped numbers for potential future stories)

++++++++++++++++

#67.   YOUNG JESUS AND JOHN VISIT ONE OF THE WISE MAN (Fiction) August 2020.

Young Jesus told John He had received an answer to a letter He had written to one of the Wise Men who had visited when Jesus was born. He told John that one had given Mary his signet ring and papers telling how to find each of them.

Jesus said, "So, if they knew of My birth, what else must they know that affects each of our futures. They can teach us much. The letter invites me to come with haste for a visit. I want you to go with Me. We leave in the morning."

John: Are you sure you want me to go?

Jesus: Yes. You are in the wilderness and study the stars more than I do and you have already prophesied things to Me. And our futures are definitely linked. Whatever we learn from this Wise Man will impact both of us.

Next morning they left early—with Mary giving each a long hug—knowing that things would be different when they returned. She of course sent along some baked goods for their host plus sandwiches for the trip. They still managed an early getaway.

After a long journey they arrived and were greeted warmly.

They discussed many things. One was Moses' writings in Genesis of God's creation. The Wise Man had some issues with things being done in a "day" until Jesus said "Jehovah's day might be 1,000 years or a million or a billion years".

Later the Wise Man said, "Maybe Jehovah created earth for mankind. If so, He had to create the moon and sun and the other planets to keep things balanced in the heavens. And even the vast millions of stars when He said "Let there be Light!" Is it possible He created everything for mankind? That is the most humbling thought I've ever had! All this for us. And what do we do with what He gave us? Jehovah must be very sad and disappointed with us. But He must love us so much because He sent You Jesus, His Son. I must stop and meditate on that."

(Later) Wise Man: I see things in the stars. I see many things but they are confusing. You will do things never done before.   John you will be revered as a prophet. Crowds will follow you as you proclaim the Messiah. Yet you will be imprisoned. Why? Jesus, multitudes will follow You and hear your teachings—love Jehovah, repent, love your neighbor, forgive, help others, peace, share, do good—wonderful messages—yet You too will be imprisoned. How could anyone not love the messages you two bring?

Jesus: They love their power and their money and they fear Rome.

Wise Man: Jesus, I see You in the stars---You are a King but have no castle, no earthly kingdom. You have no army but countless followers. You are killed—yes You die but You live on—how can that be? Other kings come and go and are forgotten but You will be remembered and worshipped forever.

Jesus: John and I will start our ministries soon. The political climate, the synagogue, Rome will never be ready—the time will never be perfect. The people need to know that Jehovah loves them. The time draws closer. You have helped us understand many things and we thank you.

Wise Man: I have learned much in these days talking with you two. Yet, there is much I do not understand—perhaps not in this life—maybe in the next. I do know John you will become the mighty prophet you were born to be, you will do the work of Jehovah and prepare the way for the Messiah. Jesus, (kneeling) I knew at Your birth You were the new King for Israel, and I know now You are the Son of Jehovah, the Messiah and Savior of the entire world and I ask You into my heart and to welcome me into your heavenly kingdom in the stars.

Jesus: Arise, we will be together forever, my Wise One.

+++++++++

John and Jesus were silent during the day as they rode the camels given to them. They were deep in thought, prayer, and resolve. As they camped that night, they discussed what they had learned and its impact on their future. The Wise Man had clarified many things and taught them much. They realized the time was drawing close for them to start their missions.

(End)

+++++++++++++++++++++++

#68. YOUNG JESUS AND JOHN—LAST TRIP TOGETHER TO THE DESERT (Fiction) Aug 2020

Jesus and John each knew this to be the final time the two of them would be alone together in the wilderness. They spent several days in deep prayer, meditation, fasting, and communion with Jehovah. The scriptures came alive more and more each day. Each could almost hear the voices of the lost calling. The Time was almost upon them. They planned, discussed and listened for Jehovah's guidance. Finally each was at peace—each was ready to leave this place of refuge. John knew he was to go first and prepare the people for the coming of Jesus—he was now ready. He would have preferred to stay in the quiet and seclusion of his beloved wilderness but he knew he had a heavenly calling for which he had been preparing all his life. As they left, John looked around and nodded as if quietly and gladly accepting the honor of the mantle Jehovah now placed upon him.

They left together, walking in silence, until they came to a fork in the trail.   John turned and said, "You are my earthly cousin, my brother in heart, and fellow adventurer.   We have met some wonderful people and learned so much from them and they helped prepare us.   Now I become the one preparing the people for the coming of You the Messiah.   Now, Jesus You are my Lord and Master and Savior and My Messiah, the long awaited Messiah, the Son of David and SON OF GOD!   I will do my best.   The world needs You and Your message. May Jehovah always protect and keep You, My Beloved Jesus."

As they hugged, John said, "You are closer to me than a brother. I know what the scriptures say will happen to the Messiah.   I would gladly take Your place if it were permitted.   But only You can do what You must do.   May Your Father always hold You close as I know He will."

Jesus said, "John, thank you.   You are one of the few who understands.   As for your mission, you will not fail.   I could not do my mission without you.   May Jehovah always give you strength.   John, you are my beloved brother in heart and soul."

And they took separate forks in the trail as they went forth and changed the world with love.

(End)

++

#69.   JESUS AT HIS 30TH BIRTHDAY.   (Fiction) August 2020

On Jesus' 30th birthday, Mary (now a grandmother) insisted on the traditional sweet bread (we call a birthday cake) and his sisters insisted on presents for everyone. So the clan gathered to celebrate and enjoy Mary's cooking and recounting the events of Jesus' remarkable birth. Jesus was swarmed by His little nieces and nephews of whom He couldn't get enough. Later He gave each a carved figure He had made just for them—a couple immediately used them as teething rings, bringing laughs all round. There was much reminiscing and even some singing and lots of laughter.

During a lull, in a serious voice, Jesus told everyone that their cousin John had been at his mission some time and was widely recognized as a prophet and was now called John the Baptist because he baptized those who repented and turned to Jehovah. Jesus went on to say that this would be His last birthday celebration with the family because He too would be starting His mission and He would see very little of any of them again. His time had come and He must now be about His heavenly Father's business.

Jesus looked at His mother and saw the knowing tears in her eyes—the long awaited day had come—her very special First Born was going forth into the world to change the world and make it better—as the angels proclaimed to the shepherds long ago, to seek to bring Peace on Earth, Good Will to all Men. Mary whispered a prayer, "Go with Jehovah My Son—My Precious Son. You are ready!"

(End)

++++++++++++++++++

++++++++++++++++++++++++++

#70.   JESUS IN MY DREAM (TRUE)   July 2020 RELATIONSHIP

I recently had an interesting dream—not sure of the exact words I spoke. Jesus held my hand as He was taking me to heaven—the Hallelujah chorus played   I said I don't want to go yet but if it's time forgive me and take me to heaven. He released my hand as I woke up. It was a comforting dream.

Don't remember if I have ever dreamed of Jesus before.

+++++++++++++

Comment: In a relationship, the distance between two people is controlled by each person.

The distance between God and a person is controlled by the person. <u>God never moves.</u>

+++++++++++++

My prayer to help the USA: DEAR LORD, HELP US LOVE YOU MORE.

+++++++++++++++++++++++

#71.   CORN   STORAGE   IN-GROUND—OLD MEMORY (True) July 2020

My friend Kathy and I were driving toward Montezuma, GA when we saw a large field of corn being harvested. (With Covid-19, we took very few trips and they were short—bathroom controlled ha ha.) We sat and watched for several hours—it was fascinating and educational. There were two cutters/mowers/harvesters that mowed the corn, shredded stalk, husk, corn, everything, and shot it into a special trailer pulled by a tractor. When full another tractor would be ready to move into place. The full trailer would be pulled to a waiting semi-trailer and the special trailer would use hydraulic power to lift the trailer high enough to empty its load into the waiting truck trailer which would hold two dumps. Everything was well coordinated—very little wasted effort. We estimated about 70-80 semi-trailers were filled that day. Very expensive equipment. That is a lot of shredded corn—and that was just one field. The field looked like a big lawn mower had cut everything. There were two cutters, seven tractors/dumpers and lots of semi-trailers. We got a small sample of the shredded corn and it had ground up corn so no corn on the cob for humans. This must be cattle/horse feed. By the way, there were lots—probably 80-100 cattle-Egrets eagerly flying in and around the harvesting equipment catching bugs or eating corn—they had a feast.

We wondered where all that mulched/shredded corn was stored or maybe shipped. We thought too much for silos. Then I remembered when a teenager, a land owner, cattle owner, Mr. Murray had employees dig a big trench(es) in the side of a hill and had ground up corn or maybe hay stored there until the cattle needed it. (Or was it on a hillside near Byron? Fuzzy memory.) Think it was covered by dirt? Wonder how they kept it from mildewing or rotting?

Another couple men were driving tractors harrowing/plowing up the recently cut field—they don't waste any time.

+++++++++++++++++++++++++++

#72. JOE LIGHTSEY—VIETNAM VET AND QUIET HERO (True) Aug 2020

Hello from Donnie, (Joe is my brother in law, Delores' younger brother. Stuart is his son. This is an email to both.)

Background: Think you saw on facebook that Rylee had a wreck --she and Haven not hurt PTL!!. The car was 2002 Camry. I got everything out of the car today at the towing place and one thing I forgot was in there was a 3 foot long crow bar (also heard it called a pinch bar). I put it in the car years ago when Joe told about (this may bring up some unpleasant memories) the time he and coworkers saw a car crash into a bridge and catch on fire. Joe, yall were able to save the lady driver and one of her children/grandchildren but not the second one. You said after that you made sure you had tools to get the doors open. And that's why I put the crow bar in the Camry, just in case I needed to get a car door open one day. Today, the crow bar triggered a memory.

And, Joe you got an award for your efforts which endangered your life. You won't call them heroic but I will. Think you said you regretted not being able to save both children but the lady thanked you/yall for saving one. The Award was I think a state of Alabama award (with money).

Comments: I've recorded Lightsey memories and tales in some of my self published books--"Powell's #2 Miscellaneous Thoughts and Stories 2020" (Pages 115-

215) (on Amazon). But I just looked and I failed to record that story Joe. I also did not record any of your Vietnam stories. Which leads to the homework assignment.

HOMEWORK: Joe and Stuart, would you video and type the story of the burning car rescue and Vietnam stories. And if you would like for me to include them in my next book (Misc...#3), email them to me.

THOUGHTS: Joe, this in a small way will help document just a little the awesome person you have always been-- something your grandchildren can read about when they get older.

++++++++++++++++++++++

<u>#73. MY BAPTISM (True) Aug 2020</u>

When I was in about the fifth grade, I gave my life to Jesus Christ and was baptized in the First Baptist Church in Buena Vista, Georgia. The baptismal pool was under the pulpit and when enough members were ready to be baptized, they would fill the pool with water (cold I think), the preacher would (I believe) put on a white robe, enter the pool and then we (I think wearing white robes) would come one by one to the pool. I guess they had put down tarps to keep the carpet dry and had told us to bring towels and extra clothing. The person in front of me (Earl Brannon) took a big gulp of air just before the preacher immersed him. (Don't remember the preacher's name.) Then it was my turn. I stepped down into the pool, the preacher turned me around, put his hands on me and said "I baptize you in the name of the Father, the Son and the Holy Ghost" (or something like that) and dunked me under, symbolizing the washing away of my sins and my devotion of my life to Jesus. I have been far from perfect but have always known that my most fundamental beliefs are these: GOD IS. JESUS IS THE LIVING SON OF THE LIVING GOD. JESUS LOVES ME. JESUS IS MY LORD AND SAVIOR WHO DIED FOR MY SINS. JESUS WILL TAKE ME TO HEAVEN WHEN I DIE. I LOVE JESUS, GOD AND THE HOLY SPIRIT WHO LOVE ME INFINITELY MORE THAN I CAN COMPREHEND. THANK YOU.

++++++++++++++++++++++++++++++++++

++++++++++++++++++++

#74.   ALWAYS ASK THE QUESTION.   June 2020 (True) (PPP Stopper list exception)

When I worked in Headquarters Air Force Reserve Civilian Personnel, we would sometimes receive a (dreaded) "Congressional Inquiry" which always had a short response time. One pertained to asking the Congressman's help in getting an exception to a regulation. She was an Air Reserve Technician (ART), a civilian employee whose job required that they attain and maintain an active Reserve membership on a job comparable to their civilian job. That meant they must be in the Air Force Reserve Unit, wear the uniform, and be ready, willing, and able to "go to war".

Background: Some Reserve Units were downsizing (probably due to changing from one aircraft to another). The surplus employees were registered in the Department of Defense (DOD) Priority Placement Program (PPP). It is also known as the "Stopper List" because it stops placement if the surplus skill matches a vacancy at another installation. The lady who wrote the Congressional was a surplus ART in a unit in Indiana and wanted to be placed in a vacant ART job in North Carolina but the vacancy was blocked by a Stopper List match. Sadly, her husband had terminal cancer and his family lived in the North Carolina area and could provide support during his final days.

When I read the Congressional, my heart went out to her, but I had read the PPP manual and attended classes—there were no such exceptions. I checked the manual again—nothing. I started preparing the negative response but decided to call the PPP office just to be sure. When I explained the situation, he said, "Contrary to popular belief, we do have a heart. Write up the request with the doctor's prognosis and get it to us and we will grant an exception". I think I said, "Have I got the right number?' I was shocked and delighted. In short order, I had the documents and confirmed with the gaining commander that he would accept her and everything worked out. I was glad I could do a small part to help that family as they went through probably the most difficult time of their life.

(PS—And had I not called and someone higher up did call PPP and got the exception, wouldn't I have looked dumb—and gotten chewed out.)

Note: Always ask the question—the worst they can say is "no"—but at least you tried.

+++

#75. JOB HOPPER June 2020 (True)

When I worked in base-level Staffing, one of my jobs was to prepare promotion certificates with up to 15 candidates for one vacancy. That resulted in one happy employee and

14 unhappy ones. After one supervisor had made a selection, he came to see me saying one of those not selected was planning to file a grievance. I said I'd look at his official records and see if I saw anything that might help—I rather doubted it but it was worth checking. I took notes of the various jobs he had held and the dates and saw a pattern. The supervisor saw my notes and quickly said "a job hopper". He came back later and thanked me over and over. Said he told the man he needed someone that would stay in the organization and work to make it stronger and better not be job hopping at the first opportunity, etc. The man withdrew his grievance. After that, at work, I had a "friend for life" and I was just doing my job—checking out a long shot but in this case it paid off. (PS Nobody needed to know the supervisor got the information after he made the selection—but since he knew people I suspect he followed his instincts and the information I provided just substantiated his judgment.)

+++++++++++++++++++

#76. I NEED MY EDUCATION. (True) By Donnie Powell June 2020

In 1961/1962, when I was a junior/senior in high school, there were discussions of closing some schools to prevent integration. The local banker, Mr. Sonny Duncan, was a member of the Georgia Highway Board in Atlanta and gave me a ride (thanks Dad for arranging that) to Atlanta to have some allergy tests (yep very allergic to tree and grass pollens, house dust, etc.). During the drive, he asked me what I thought about school closings. I told him I did not want our schools to close because I needed my education— that I was not strong or mechanically skilled like my brothers. I planned to go to college and probably couldn't if our schools closed. He thought awhile and told me if I needed help (implied financial) going to college, to come see him. (When at Georgia Southern, I did go see him for a loan on a used Falcon—Dad co-signed the loan--thanks again Dad—and Mr. Sonny.) Our Marion County schools did remain open. (I'm sure what I said had no impact but I was and am thankful that our leaders kept the schools open.)

+++++++++++++++++++++

#77. MEMORIES BY RYLEE FOR O+PA JUNE 2020

Memories   by   Rylee Hancock

(I tried my best to put these in chronological order from earliest to most recent)

21 Jun 2020 Father's Day –Gift to O+PA

June 11, 2004 – Before Haven was born, I remember telling mom and dad that I would teach her to play hopscotch. I didn't think she would be a baby. I thought she would be my age immediately. June 11 will always have a special place in my heart because it's the day that my best friend Haven was born! I remember waiting at Oma and Opa's house while my mom and dad were at the hospital awaiting her arrival. Oma and Opa were asking me all sorts of questions like "Are you excited to meet your sister?" When she was born, we went to the hospital and I remember the waiting room having a spot for kids to play. I remember it being blue with fish on the wall, and chairs. I think I was playing a game like bus stop or something. When it was finally time to go in and see Haven, I remember faintly holding her for the first time and saying "She's perfect."

Little Rylee – Going to Oma and Opa's house was always an adventure. One thing my Opa did to entertain me was place my stuffed animals on the printer and print pictures of them. I thought it was the coolest thing ever! I had pictures of my favorites, Wawa and Bunny Bun.

Little Rylee (age 2-3) – Our first pet was named NinJa, and we had him until he died a few years ago at the age of 15. (He was about 6 months old when we adopted him) I remember being in the cat adoption area of PetSmart and seeing mom hold the little black blob. He nestled into her neck and didn't want her to let go. We debated naming him Magic, but settled with NinJa, with a capital J. I remember being worried about him when we moved into the new house. I was afraid he was upset in the old house by himself. When dad picked me up to look into the room which is now the playroom, I remember asking "What about NinJa?" Also moving into the new house, I remember when we walked in for the first time and the little girl playing with her toy house. When it was time to move in, I remember riding in mom's car with a mattress strapped onto the back.

Little Rylee (maybe 4) – Once at Oma and Opa's house mom was holding me and walked up to a chair that had their old cat, Zoe, in it. I asked her to move the cat before she sat down. Mom said, "Sit on her or move her?" I exclaimed, "No don't sit on her, MOVE HER!" then giggled. Safe to say I've always cared about animals. Zoe must have heard us talking because she quickly jumped down after that.

Little Rylee (around 5-6) – We fostered kittens. A lot. I remember one of our first batch of kittens was around 14 years ago. They were all grey and adorable. Dad has Haven and I in the bath and I heard mom come in and exclaim, "Come on out I have a surprise for you!" I came out and saw a cage with a bunch of little eyes staring back at me. There were 5 kittens in total. The kitten in the front was the spunkiest and fluffiest. We named him Pinkerton and we still have him today. They stayed in my mom and dad's room when we first got them and would hide behind their dresser. One was more skittish than the rest and would hardly come out. There would also be two piles of sleepy kittens at the end of the bed. I remember getting to have two kittens in my room one time. I put them in my dresser drawer. I'd open one drawer, then they'd be in a different one. I think I might have dropped one on accident because I remember being told I couldn't have them in my room anymore. Oops. In the mornings, early, around 6am, I would go into the playroom and it was just an ocean of kittens. There was a large mattress propped up against the wall and sitting on top was our old cat Gina. I would climb up there with her as the kittens jumped and tried to grab my feet. There were maybe ten kittens all running around. Names that I remember were Panda, Marshmallow, Bam Bam, Liberty, and of course Pinkerton.

Little Rylee (maybe age 6-7) – I loved the Baby Einstein series. I went to a friend's house once and somehow, we got on the subject of those dvds. I asked if she still had them and she said she had gotten rid of them. (I had not yet outgrown them) I went home and put some dvds in a bag to give her because I wanted her to be able to watch them too. Mom explained that she had outgrown them and so her mom got rid of them. I kept the dvds and continued watching them for the next several years.

Young Rylee (maybe 7-8) – After the porch was out in and mats were installed, dad brought home a bunch of cardboard from work. He set up a maze and we would run around and try not to let him catch us. We would also ride our bikes around and set up a shop. Lots of laughter as we would purposely ride into the wall to get dad's reaction. We also had swings on the porch. We came up with lots of things to do, such as the 'Let Go', which is where dad would bring us up as high as he could then let go of us. He would also spin us around while we were on our bellies and we'd go so fast.

Young Rylee (maybe age 7-10) – Opa taught me how to type. I remember sitting at his computer showing off my typing skills. I would learn by watching him too. I was so impressed by how fast he could type and with little to no errors. I would speak a sentence and he would type it out for me as fast as he could. I think I was writing a story about a chicken and a husband and wife? Not sure what was going on but I remember always being excited to type on his big computer.

Little/Young/Preteen Rylee – Ping pong in the hallway. Not sure how this got started but it sure was a hit! Lots of laughter and smiles every time we did this. Something else we did at Oma and Opa's house was pay vet. We had exam rooms set up and of course Opa had plenty of stuffed animals for us to pay with. We would print out labels for medications and would drive around on our bikes. That was always a huge hit, riding bikes through the house, and it was incorporated into most of our activities. Sometimes we'd just ride around and sing songs.

+++++++++++++++++++

#78 Our little POPPY GIRL   Sept 10, 2020

(A little song/prayer while waiting to hear that she was born and ok. Didn't know her name was Lily.)

Thank you Lord for our little Poppy Girl,

You brought her into this world.

She brought a smile to her mom and dad,

Thank You for our Poppy Girl.

Who will make the world a happier place.

Thank you Lord for our little Poppy Girl.

She will make everyone in the world

Smile when they think about this Poppy Girl.

Thank you Lord for our little Poppy Girl.

+++
++++

#79 A daily prayer: OH LORD: HELP ME TO LOVE YOU MORE. Etc. Sep 2020

LOVE MATTERS.

+++++++++

Hate can justify anything.

++++++++++++++

<u>#80. MOVING A METAL CARPORT (True) Oct 2020</u>

Background: At our home on Wake Forest Drive in Warner Robins, I had a 20 foot by 20 foot metal carport installed over our driveway. Why did I get a carport? Why not just park in the garage? When our daughter Sharon moved out, she left her cats with us and their litter boxes were in the garage, so I could not park in the garage. I could go through the garage to unload groceries, etc., because the loud noise of the garage door opening terrified the cats and they flew through the cat door into the house. The carport helped keep me from getting wet. But I wanted to move it closer to the garage and this led to a "Donnie Project"

The carport was about 8-10 feet away from the house. It was outside the sidewalk leading to the front door because there is a two inch metal support pipe running the length of the carport and people would trip over it if it were on top of the sidewalk. But if I tried to move the carport the tripping problem would exist. Finally decided I could cut/chip/hammer a two inch trench across the three foot wide sidewalk. (Later realized I could have rented a saw to cut the concrete.) Cutting the concrete was tough. Bought a hand chisel tool that I hit with a hammer and made some progress. Later got my bigger 6 pound sledge hammer with an axe on one end and hammered away making faster progress. Finally, with much determination got the trench completed. The second project required the help of my son Ben. But first had to use ropes to tie the vertical support posts to each other to keep the whole thing from collapsing inward or outward.   Then had to use a crow bar to pull the 18 inch long metal anchors out. Next used shovel as a lever to raise each end of the carport and put some sort of pipes/rollers/cylinders under it, to make it easier to push into place. Finally we were ready to push the carport—which probably weighed several hundred pounds—into place. Ben on one side and me on the other—outside in the clear—safe—we hoped. I told him, "If it starts fall, run." (Yes we had moved the cars. I think.) Three, two, one—we pushed and surprise, the carport moved and rolled right into place—within a couple of feet of the house. Used shovel to lift, while Ben removed pipes all the way around, a little pushing it fit into the trench—sidewalk safe no tripping there—hammered the anchors into place and everything worked as I hoped. (Hope I thanked Ben.) Surprise, surprise, a Donnie project that worked. Thanks Ben.

+++

#81. RAISING A SMALL METAL SHED (True) Oct 2020

My wife Delores and I put together an 8 foot by 10 foot metal shed that required hundreds of nuts and bolts—her on one side and me on the other. It lasted for years but the metal door was five feet high which meant I often bumped my head. Years later, finally came up with a Donnie project—I devised a way to raise the shed about 8 inches. I took a number of steps, some before, during and after the day I raised the shed. Bought an outside door at a yard sale, attached to a 4" by 4" treated post (should have poured cement around it since it later leaned to one side). Unscrewed the bolts anchoring the shed to the cement cap blocks. Had 8" cement blocks on hand and some 2" by 4" sections to use to raise the shed in increments. Used shovel to lift a part of the shed, slip a 2 x 4 under it, move lift slip a 2 x 4, etc., until entire shed was lifted 4". Then lifted around again until entire shed was lifted 8" and able to put

8" cement blocks all the way around. Anchored corners. Poured sand in spaces in blocks to keep critters out. Used metal saw-blade to cut threshold of metal shed. Covered a few open spaces to keep critters out. Checked everything. No longer bumped my head—more headroom in shed. Surprise, surprise. This Donnie project seemed to have worked.

(Note: I don't tell about my projects that did not work. Ha ha)

+++++++++++++++++++++++++++++++++++

#82.   PUSHING   BATTERY-POWERED WHEELCHAIR—GOD'S TIMING (True) 2 Oct 2020

Kathy and I had just finished our walk around Walker's Pond when we noticed our acquaintances were not moving. The young girl, always with a happy attitude, in her battery-powered wheelchair was waiting as her middle aged female care giver stood beside her. We noticed they had moved a little distance up the small hill since we last saw them. As we prepared to leave it dawned on us that the batteries were not working and the caregiver was trying her best to push the very heavy wheelchair up the challenging incline and eventually home. Because of Covid-19 we were reluctant to help but we could not just leave them— there was nobody else around to assist them. We had masks on and there were extra gloves in the car and Kathy declined to wait in the car so we walked over and offered our assistance, which they gladly accepted. Did I say small hill? It was a mountain. And battery powered wheel chairs weigh as much as a tank. I pushed it a short distance and sweet wonderful Kathy asked if she could take over and I— feeling no masculine pride at all—gladly (and humbly) said

"Yes". We alternated and joked with the young girl about us exceeding the speed limit and things like that. Total distance was only about 500 yards (thank goodness) when the caregiver said she could take over because they were almost home. (Kathy helped me back to the car. Just joking.) We had been careful and glad we helped because the caregiver could not have done it by herself.

When I got home, it finally hit me that God timed it just right—to the minute—so Kathy and I would be there when they needed us. He nudged us to notice they weren't moving and that they needed help. He had placed us there at that precise time to help them. Had we been there 10 minutes earlier or later we probably would not have noticed the situation or would not have seen them. His timing was just right. So—nudge, nudge, go help and we did. I am always amazed at God's timing. Thank you Lord. (End)

(Note: Names of our walking acquaintances withheld since I do not have their permission.)

(Note 2: In this time of many people saying negative things about race relations, we are of different races— things like this happen every day—we are all God's children.)

+++++++++++++++++++++++++

#83.   MY HAIR IS LONGER THAN YOURS! YAAAH! PRAISE THE LORD!   (True) Sep 2020

The 45 or so year old daughter often visits her mother, my neighbor. When she told me she had cancer and was undergoing radiation/chemo I gave her one or two stuffed animals and wished her a quick recovery saying when she was well she could give a stuffed animal to someone who was going through similar treatment. Her hair fell out but when she came to visit her mom, I'd wish her well and through the months, I'd inquire from her mom how she was doing. She recovered completely praise the Lord. Then the other day when she visited her mom, she waived, fluffed her 3-4 inch hair and said "My hair is longer than yours now!" And we both shouted "Yaaah. Praise the Lord!" Made me smile. What a blessing.

+++++++++++++++++++++

#84. MISS VERNA ALLISON - My favorite teacher By Jack Christopher (True) Oct 2020

(Used with Jack's permission—see below)

MISS VERNA ALLISON - My favorite teacher   By Jack Christopher

I never experienced Mrs. Moss' class but had the distinct pleasure of being a student of Miss Verna Allison for 3 years of grammar school. The first years included grades 4 and 5 which took place in a little 2 room Schoolhouse in Tazewell, Ga. It was actually one large room with a divider in the middle which accommodated grades 1 through 3 in one section taught by Mrs. Chloe Croxton and grades 4 through 6 in the other section being taught by Miss Verna Allison. There was also a small kitchen/dining room off to the side which served some outstanding country dinners (we referred to lunch as dinner back then). These meals were prepared by Mrs. Elizabeth McCorkle, wife of Jabez McCorkle who drove the school bus for many years from Tazewell to Buena Vista. Quite often these meals were prepared using fresh vegetables from her garden or from one of the many gardens of other generous Tazewell neighbors. Since this was a time before the advent of indoor plumbing, there was also a modest 2 – hole outhouse situated slightly behind and away from the main Schoolhouse. This Schoolhouse still stands and serves as a Community Center for the citizens of Tazewell.

This schoolhouse was heated by two large pot-bellied stoves that were located in the center of each room. These heaters were fueled by coal that was stored outside in a pile near the side entrance. One of the duties of the male students was to periodically replenish the coal bucket whenever it became empty. No one ever complained about these duties since most of us were performing the same duties at home.

Our water supply was powered by a windmill near the coal pile that pumped water into a holding tank. We didn't use much water back then since our toilet was located in the outhouse and did not have running water. We were sometimes asked to carry a bucket or two of water into the kitchen for Mrs. McCorkle.

There was another small room off the main section called the "Cloak Room" which was used to store our coats in the wintertime. It also served as a "Time Out" detention area where we would be banished to whenever we misbehaved or committed some other offense during class. This was also the area where we would be subjected to a more severe punishment for offenses of a more serious nature. This involved a "whooping" or paddling administered to the rear end by Miss Allison with her favorite disciplinary device which was a large wooden paddle that she always referred to as the "Board of Education". I must have been one of her favorite students because I remember quite a few visits with her into the Cloak Room with the Board of Education"

While most of my visits to the Cloak Room were justified, there was one that I have to this day considered to have been a major miscarriage of justice. In the small town of Tazewell it was customary for us to go barefoot starting in the springtime and continuing throughout the summer. This was also allowed in school and most of us really looked forward to the time when we could toss the shoes and run around barefoot all day until the end of the school term and the rest of the summer.

In this particular situation, unbeknownst to me the removal of shoes was permitted only after an official date that was determined by the teacher in charge. It was early spring and since we were already going barefoot at home with the permission of my parents, I naturally assumed that it was also OK at school. I remember that day quite well. It was springtime and a little cooler that morning so I wore my shoes to school as usual. It got much warmer during the day and when recess time came around it had turned into a very warm summer day. Since I had the permission of my parents I could not resist and off went the shoes. This did not remain unnoticed by Miss Allison who promptly escorted me into the Cloak Room for a vigorous session with her and the Board of Education. I tried to explain that my parents had given me permission but that fell on deaf ears. Looking back, I guess that was my first introduction to conflicting rules of conduct that might apply differently in different situations. Back then we respected all of our teachers and never questioned anything they said or did. Our parents shared the same respect for teachers, in fact one of the common conventions back then was "If you get a whooping at school, it is not over because you will surely get another when you get home".

Miss Allison was a devout Cristian who did not hesitate to share her Christian beliefs with her students, which was perfectly acceptable at that time. We always had to recite the Pledge of Allegiance every day of school and often the Lord's Prayer as well. She taught us quite a few Hymns such as "Onward Christian Soldiers", "Swing Low, Sweet Chariot", and "Amazing Grace". I remember several occasions when she would take us on a short visit to a local elderly person who was very ill or near death and we would gather around and sing those Hymns for them. They always seemed to enjoy our serenades.

Miss Allison also had us memorize numerous religious poems and prayers. Among those were "Abou Ben Adam" and "A Tribute to Christ", not to mention some bible verses such as the 23rd Psalm.

There weren't many students in Miss Allisons' classes in Tazewell. The ones I remember are Brenda O'Hearn, Paul Harbuck, Billy McElmurray, Gloria McCorkle, Karen Welch, and Judy Halley.

Shortly after the 5th grade, the Tazewell school was closed and we had to take the bus to Buena Vista for the rest of our grammar school years. Miss Allison also moved to the Buena Vista school and taught me in the 7th grade which was in a basement room located underneath the grammar school. I distinctly remember that when it rained heavily, sometimes the lower walkway into the schoolroom would flood and we might have to walk through some standing water to get to class.

I also remember that Miss Allison had developed a new disciplinary action to take the place of the Board of Education. I think at that time, paddling had been discontinued by the individual teachers and was turned over to the Principal's office for execution. I can distinctly remember on many occasions having to write "I will not talk in class" over a hundred times on the blackboard until it was completely filled up. I thought I was pretty smart and started gradually writing my sentence with larger letters to take up more space but Miss Allison caught up with that trick in no time and made me erase what I had done and start over.

On a more personal note, Miss Allison had a sister who died of cancer at an early age, leaving behind two little boys name Chap and Charles Stevens. Miss Allison told us that she had made a promise to her dying sister that she would take care of those two boys. She honored that promise, never married and looked after those boys as if they were her own. She was always talking about Chap and Charles throughout the school year and I could tell that she was completely dedicated to those 2 boys.

I am not sure what happened to Miss Allison later in life but do remember that she had to give up her teaching job because she was living in the same house as the two boys and their Father which was not proper back in those days. I am sure of one thing and that is that she would never have done anything unethical or immoral in any situation whatsoever. She was merely keeping her promise to her sister and was willing to give up her profession that she dearly loved in order to do so. To me that is one of the greatest sacrifices that a true Christian can make by placing the welfare of others above one's self in order to keep a solemn promise made years ago.

In spite of all of our misunderstandings and disciplinary situations, I still regard Miss Allison as the best and most influential teacher that I have ever had the pleasure of being taught by. She was a very stern, honest, dedicated, faithful Christian teacher of the highest degree who taught me many life lessons that I still abide by to this day and will continue to do so. She was truly a wonderful, caring teacher and a beautiful human being.

++++++++++++++++++++

Ok to send anywhere you choose. This started out as just a couple of sentences but once I got started, old memories just kept pouring in. It is just sad that teaching has seemed to have gotten corrupted just like most everything else. Who would want to become a teacher or police officer these days? Things were a lot simpler and saner back then. We didn't have much but we were much better off.   Jack

++++++++++++++

Donnie, I just got the email about Mrs Moss and prayer in school and started an email response about that which has grown into quite a lengthy essay. Then I remembered that you asked about experiences growing up in Marion County which I had intended to respond to at some time but never got around to it.

Anyway I just completed it and am sending it to you in response to your initial request. This has morphed into a sort of tribute to my favorite teacher but does contain quite a bit of the grammar school experience in Tazewell, Ga.

I am inserting it below and also as a PDF attachment. I don't have a recent email list of classmates so please distribute to them or anyone else that you would like to. Jack